ZAFIRA AND THE BIRDS

By EUGENIE MAKROGIANNIS

For my parents, Therese and Nicolas,
who gave me the world and encouraged me to fly.

CONTENTS

PART ONE: THE DREAM PLANNERS

PART TWO: ZAFIRA AND THE GIRLS

PART ONE:

THE DREAM PLANNERS

CHAPTER 1: ZAFIRA AND YAYA

Zafira sprang upright, her blanket like a second pillow. She blinked and squinted until the dark mound across the room morphed into her favorite stuffed unicorn. Its tangled rainbow mane was a welcome sight.

Home.

She smiled and yawned—long and deep—then slid out of bed and dug around the floor for her shorts.

But the Minotaur was so different. She pursed her lips. *And Theseus was way shorter, and what about those columns!*

Zafira got dressed while her mind replayed details from her dream. She could still smell the dirt from the maze and feel the heat from the scorching sun.

Zafira knew she'd need to get it down fast before it slipped away. She grabbed her backpack and rushed downstairs.

Ever since she was eight years old—a whole two years ago—Zafira Panos started planning her dreams, dreaming them, remembering them when she awoke, and cataloging them in her owl-covered dream journal.

Zafira liked to get her 'archiving' done first thing in the morning and usually managed to jot down every detail while eating her Nutella-smeared bagel.

She was busy looking up how to spell 'labyrinth' when her father grabbed the tablet from her hands.

"Dad!" she groaned, reaching for the device. "I was in the middle of something!"

"Well," Stelios Panos shrugged, "you'll have to be in the middle again tonight, honey." He gulped down the last of his coffee. "We're late."

Zafira's dad was a Classics professor at the university that was the heart of their small town of Davis, California. He was short, slim, and owned every type of Lands' End sweater ever made, except for the cardigans—which he said made him look like a cliché of a cliché, explaining to Zafira that it meant being unoriginal.

Her mom always rolled her eyes when she saw her husband browsing their website, and both she and Zafira would share a chuckle when he would call out, "Look Luce, there's a sale on pullovers!"

Zafira's mom, Lucy Roberts-Panos, was taller than her husband, had a honey-colored bob, curvy features, and loved to wear layers over layers of colorful, mismatched tops on her days off. On her days on, she worked as a busy nurse administrator in a hospital in nearby Sacramento. She was often gone before Zafira and Stelios sat down for breakfast, as was the case that morning.

"But Dad, I'm almost done," Zafira pleaded. "I might forget later. We're being tested on map coordinates today, and how can you expect me to remember the *nuances* of my dream with all that x- and y- number stuff?"

"Nuances, huh?" her dad grinned. "Nice word. But up you go. Brush teeth, hair, shoes, and we're Outtie 5000."

Zafira scoffed while heading back to her room. "Outtie 5000? You always say that dad, and it sounds so dumb. What does it even mean?" But her dad was already outside.

Zafira shuffled into the driveway a few minutes later, and her dad ran behind her to lock the door.

"Oh wait! My scarf!" Zafira spun back around.

"Zaffy! It's like seventy-five. You don't need a scarf." But he was already holding the door open. There was a running joke in the family recently about how Zafira had picked up a uniquely *un*-Californian, more European sense of style from her Grandma Leni, which included accessorizing with assorted scarves and, in Zafira's words: 'Ugh, like, *neverrrrr* wearing flip-flops.'

"Come on, Zafira, hurry up!" her dad called out down the hallway. "Anyway, it's Wednesday half-day. You know you're going to Yaya's later. There'll be *lots* of scarves there."

Every Wednesday, Zafira's school, Tree Line Elementary, lets grades 1-6 out at 11:45 am. Zafira absolutely *loved* Wednesdays because she could walk over to Yaya Leni's house and stay until dinner.

Yaya Leni, or Eleni Panos as her friends and colleagues knew her, was a seventy-seven-year-old retired art historian who lived in the coolest house in all of Davis—maybe even in all of California. She was confident, independent, and a rock star in Zafira's eyes.

When she retired from teaching high school Art History in Ventura (Southern California), Yaya Leni started traveling all over Europe, Asia, and South America. She often met up with her archaeologist friends on digs in Egypt, Greece, Turkey, and Italy. Yaya Leni definitely believed in living a life full of experiences, which is why she was the one to teach Zafira how to 'plan her dream adventures.'

As her dad backed up, Zafira opened her dream journal

and smiled. She couldn't wait until noon when she'd already be walking through Yaya's red front door, ready to eat her weekly slice of *spanakopita* and listen to her grandmother's latest tale.

***

It was precisely 12:17 pm when she actually got to Yaya's house. The delay was because Zafira had walked part of the way with her friend Vivian, who had been pushing her bike and kept stopping to investigate a strange noise coming from the chain.

"Yaya!" Zafira called out as she dumped her backpack on a low bench in the front hall. "I'm here!"

"In my closet upstairs, sweetie. Grab a piece of *pita* and come on up."

Zafira bee-lined to the kitchen, picked up a napkin, and swiped two pieces of the spinach-and-cheese pie. She then headed back toward the front, where a dark, wooden staircase led upstairs.

Zafira's great-grandparents were both born in Greece and even though Yaya was born in Chicago, her two sons—Zafira's dad and Uncle 'Theo' Leo—and Zafira grew up surrounded by all-things-Greek, most importantly pans and pans of Greek main dishes glistening with olive oil and trays of honey, nutty Greek desserts.

Zafira made her way into her grandma's bedroom, which just happened to be Zafira's favorite room in her favorite house. Who wouldn't love a room that looked like a museum *and* a bookstore? Okay, probably most ten-year-olds wouldn't.

But not Zafira. She loved touching all the travel souvenirs and flipping through all the art, photography, and travel books, not to mention all those other books by people with fascinating names like Allende and Murakami—which Zafira would say out loud in her deepest, most breathy voice.

But the best part of the room was the massive, dark bamboo canopy bed that took up the entire middle of the room. Zafira went straight for it and melted into the feathery softness of the comforter.

"When you're done foam-falling, Zaffy, come on over here and give me a hand," Yaya's muffled voice called out.

'Foam-falling' was what they called lying down on fluffy blankets and imagining they were floating on top of their favorite frothy, warm milk drinks. It was Inside Joke #1052—one of many.

Zafira rolled off and found her grandma on her hands and knees, her head lost in the bottom row of hanging clothes.

"What are you doing, Yaya?"

"See that boot by the door?"

Zafira noticed a mud-caked, light-brown hiking boot.

"It's missing its partner-in-crime. And I think you're just the girl who'll find it." Yaya shimmied out backward and sat back on her heels as Zafira dove in. "Thatta girl, Zaffy. My best urban digger!"

Zafira crawled around the back of the closet, tossing out other shoes, folded paper bags, and fallen belts.

Yaya stood up. She was petite but sturdy, with her long, silver hair clipped back into a bun. She looked down at her granddaughter and smiled from her chin to her eyebrows.

Zafira kept digging while Yaya organized the clothes hanging on the opposite side of the two-sided walk-through closet.

Another reason Zafira absolutely *loved* Yaya's bedroom

was this uncommon closet, with its rows of multi-colored clothes and surprise discoveries. Even better was what the closet led to—Yaya's bathroom.

The bathroom was full of plants, orchids, fancy bottles of French shampoo, and scented candles. There was a sunken bathtub next to a gray slate shower and a small copper vanity sink in the corner. Zafira thought it looked like *The Jungle Book* but smelled like vanilla cupcakes.

"Yaya, it looks like a backyard in here," Zafira had once said.

"No, *koukla mou*, it's my little escape into a secret rainforest," Yaya had replied with a wink and a smile.

One of Zafira's favorite things was to sit—fully dressed—in the sunken bathtub, look over at the stone and wood walls, and imagine she was in a fancy hotel in a distant land waiting for a secret messenger to deliver her spy assignment.

"How was school today, sweetie?"

Zafira emerged with the rogue boot. "It was okay. But dad didn't let me finish writing in my dream journal this morning, and I can't really remember how it all ended in the maze."

"Zaffy, you do remember I told you that you shouldn't plan your dreams *every* night, right? And you don't have to be so strict about writing it all down. Where's the fun in that? It's got to stay an adventure, darling, not become a chore."

"I know, but I like it. And I *need* it." Zafira sat up, her legs stretched out in a 'V' and her arms supporting her from the back. "Yaya... It's just so sad, so boring!"

"What is, honey?"

"My life!" Zafira crumbled back, lying down. "I mean, you've been, like, *everywhere!* And Sarah Hewitt just came back from Australia over Christmas break. Pedro Guiterrez's family is planning an Alaskan wilderness vacation this summer. And Mia Platterson's family...well, they have Niels."

"And who is Niels?"

"Their exchange student from The Notterlands."

"Do you mean The Netherlands?" Yaya chuckled.

"Exactly! I mean, don't you see, Yaya? Everyone else is living these mysterious, exciting lives, and all I have are my stupid dreams. I mean, they're fun and all, but everyone dreams!"

"Well, actually, honey, I don't think everyone can *plan* their dreams. We've got a special little gift, you and I."

"Nah, I'm sure if they really put their minds to it, they could, too. See, Yaya, it's not that special. It's cool, but...where's the mystery? Where's the intrigue?"

Yaya snorted out a laugh.

Zafira rolled onto her side and started twirling a hanging scarf. "I know, I know, you think I'm being silly, like you always say," she sighed in protest. "Just...can you tell me about Brazil again? Or maybe Italy? Or someplace else?"

"Zaffy—"

Zafira scrambled up, kneeling.

"Oh, but wait!" she interrupted. "Can you first tell me the story about Aria...Ariadna?"

"Ariadne," Yaya corrected her.

"Yeah, Ariadne again? I got to the part where she gave the demi-god Theseus a ball of thread to help him escape the Minotaur's labyrinth. But in my dream, the Minotaur didn't have the head of a bull and the body of a man like you had said. He had our neighbor's dog Lucky's body, and the face of that guy on that *Jeopardy* show you always like to watch."

Yaya laughed. "Well, I know people sometimes think Alex Trebek's been around forever, but I'm sure he wasn't around in ancient Greece!" Yaya stood up and dusted off her yoga pants. "Come on, kiddo. I think I'm done with the closet for today. Tea time?"

CHAPTER 2: STATUES AND TEMPLES

Zafira dipped her second chocolate chip cookie into the steamy mug of tea and skimmed the art history book Yaya had grabbed on their way to the kitchen. She tossed the pages around, jumping from stiff-looking Egyptian statues to dark churches to weird paintings with swirly lines.

"Oh, sweetie, you must get so bored of your dad and me always talking about all this old art and mythology stuff," Yaya said while cutting up vegetables for a salad. "Let's leave Ariadne for a while. Why don't you tell me what you and Vivian talked about today?"

"Ugh! Viv wouldn't stop talking about how she's going to get her hair cut this weekend," Zafira grumbled. She flipped the pages faster. "I mean, it's all so boring. Who cares?"

"I'm sure *she* cares, and I bet she'd care if you changed your hair," Yaya said.

Zafira pulled a strand from her poufy, dark curls. "Eww! You know there's no hope for this mess!"

Zafira was tall, thin, freckled, and didn't look like

9

anyone else in the family. In fact, she was secretly convinced she was probably adopted since she didn't have a good memory, like Yaya and her dad, and had no creative skills like her mom. Her most distinguishing feature was the mass of hair on her head.

Her mom and Yaya envied it, and her dad and Theo Leo said it made her the most beautiful girl in the world. Zafira thought it made her look like she had an overgrown alpaca head.

Zafira flicked the strand, frowned, and looked down. "Well, it's not that I *don't* care about Viv, really. It's just... I don't know..." She came to a picture of a Greek temple. "See? Look, this is what I'm talking about."

Yaya craned her neck to get a look. "Oh yes. The Parthenon."

"Exactly! The Parthenon! The Acropolis! I totally remember our trip last summer. It was the *best*! You held my hand so I wouldn't slip on those slippery marble steps, and it was *so* hot I thought my head would explode. And then when we got up to the top, I saw that huge temple... I want that! I mean, I want to see things like that every day, visit cool places, and take planes all over. And *not* be stuck in Mrs. Dyson's boring class all day long."

Yaya laughed. "*Agape mou*, you will. I promise you will. Just be patient. Everything comes with time." Yaya popped a cherry tomato into her mouth.

"When I was ten, I never thought I would even *see* a plane up close, let alone ride in one," Yaya continued. "I was stuck in a classroom once, too. We didn't have a TV yet, computers didn't exist, and I played with the ugliest dolls. Plus, I didn't even know how to plan my dreams back then. Talk about dull!"

Yaya sat down next to Zafira and stroked her forearm.

"You are so, so lucky, sweetie. I wish you could see that."

Zafira scoffed and rolled her eyes.

Yaya went back to the cutting board. "Oh Zafira, you'll see that your problems aren't so tragic one day. And while you might be the center of *our* universe...oh, honey, you are most definitely not the center of *the whole* universe."

Zafira sighed while Yaya scraped the veggies into a wooden bowl. Then, in a quiet voice, she said, "Yaya, I know I've already asked for a million different stories today, but I know now what I'd like to talk about. Can you tell me the stuff you told me...like that day on the Acropolis? About the columns and stuff? I want to remember how it was when we were in that ancient place, far away. Like, I just want to be back there."

Yaya wiped her hands on a towel, an indulgent smile on her face. She sat down beside Zafira and pointed to the photo of the temple. Then, in her calmest, most soothing voice, she began talking.

"Do you see how these columns are square on top, hon? Those are called Doric, and they are the simplest of the three orders—or types—of Greek columns. And that big triangle on top of the temple? That's called a pediment. It was once decorated with these beautifully carved statues."

"Those are the statues you told me they took to a museum in London, right?" Zafira leaned in, her chin resting in her hand.

"Yup. A long time ago. But today, lots of other people want them to be moved back to the Acropolis. And who knows? Maybe one day they will make their way back home." Yaya brushed a curl away from Zafira's forehead.

"Also, remember how I told you the Parthenon, and actually most of the Acropolis, didn't look like it does today?" Yaya asked.

Zafira nodded and smiled.

"Good, because back then, in a period known as Classical—which, remember honey, is only a stylistic name that means it's connected to how things *looked* at a particular time in history."

Zafira kept nodding, transfixed.

"Well, most temples and statues weren't white like today. They were decorated and painted bright primary colors. Could you imagine seeing this temple all blue and red? Even these—" Yaya pointed to a group of unsmiling statues, which the book called *korai.* "Yep, even those were all red, blue, and yellow. Even green."

"Oh yeah!" Zafira exclaimed. "I remember those girl statues in the museum we went to below the temple. Some were really funny-looking."

"Speaking of funny-looking, did I tell you about the statue of Athena last summer?"

"I don't think so. Or at least, I don't remember."

"Well, Zaffy, imagine seeing an enormous, over forty-foot-tall statue of Athena made out of gold and ivory right in the center of the Parthenon."

"No way, really?"

"Yes, that was there too, but it didn't look anything like these older Egyptian statues that began as simple versions of people with unrealistic features like huge, bulging eyes, blank faces, and arms and legs that bent in impossible ways." Yaya flipped back in the book to one of the statues Zafira had seen before.

"Instead, imagine a massive, almost gaudy, bright yellow-and-white statue staring out from the middle of the Parthenon? Wouldn't that have been intimidating but also quite a sight?"

Zafira's eyes sparkled. She'd never get tired of listening

to her grandma talk about temples and statues.

As Yaya kept going, Zafira's mind drifted back to that dusty Athenian hill surrounded by city block after city block of concrete buildings. It was crowded, noisy, and even a bit dirty, but Zafira loved how different it was from Davis.

She couldn't wait to dream about it again. Sure, since their family trip, she had planned many dreams, both in ancient and modern Athens, but they were never that much fun.

Nothing like the real deal.

Maybe, tonight, something would be different, more exciting. She could plan to go back to Classical Greece to see that huge Athena statue in the Parthenon. Even more, maybe she could meet a local—someone who could show her around and maybe even invite her over to eat. Zafira really wanted to find out what dinner was like back then. But not until she had had her own delicious dinner with Yaya first.

They ate grilled, lemon oil chicken, steamed rice, and a crunchy salad. Soon after, Zafira's mom came to pick her up, and they headed home.

Zafira zipped through her homework and bedtime routine and was already kissing her parents goodnight by nine, over an hour before her usual bedtime.

"Got a dream in mind for tonight, honey?" Zafira's mom asked.

"Mm-hmm," Zafira answered absently while picking up her school books from the coffee table.

Her mom sat in her little painting nook near the living room's bay window. She has always loved painting as a hobby since she was Zafira's age. Even though she was busy all week, she tried to squeeze in some painting time whenever possible.

While Zafira hugged her mom goodnight, she peeked at

her mom's latest portrait. Her mom took close-up photos of friends, family, and sometimes strangers and painted them with a mix of strange colors, textures, and patterns.

Tonight, she was working on a portrait of a young barista from their local Starbucks. She was painting the face cappuccino brown—with cheeks that looked like two cinnamon rolls—and gluing on espresso beans as some of the strands of the barista's dark brown hair.

"I like the beans part, mom," Zafira said and spun off.

"Just don't forget to brush your teeth," Zafira's mom called out.

"Yup! Good night." Zafira whizzed off to her room.

It was dream time!

CHAPTER 3: HEARD AND (UN)SEEN

Planning a dream was actually pretty simple, and Zafira always wondered why more people didn't do it.

First, she would lie down and stare up at the reflected stars and planets from her bedside spinning lamp. She'd gaze at the rotations and mentally focus on where she wanted to go or what she wanted to do, including where she'd start and where she'd finish.

Of course, when she actually dreamt the dream, she hardly ever ended up *exactly* where she planned. But she did get close a whole bunch of times—probably because she could actually talk to herself in her dreams and so she could sort of 'guide' herself where she needed to go. It was part of the fun—seeing if she could get where she wanted to on the first try.

The last thing Zafira would do was turn off the lights, shut her eyes, and think a word or phrase over and over until she finally fell asleep.

Then, magically, she would be transported. It worked every time, just like how her mom's chocolate caramel brownies would turn a bad day good—every time.

So, that night, as her eyelids got heavier and the reflection got fuzzier, she rolled over and thought: *Parthenon. Parthenon. Parthe—*

Zafira opened her eyes and saw she was in the middle of a deserted field. Wild plants, flower bushes, and a smattering of trees surrounded her. She glanced to her right and saw a dirt path.

She looked down to make sure she wasn't wearing anything strange. Zafira did this because she had once dreamt of being on a tropical island, but her subconscious must have got 'tropic' mixed up with 'arctic' because she had landed on the beach in a huge yellow ski parka and thick snow boots. And there was nothing worse than walking on a sandy beach with heavy boots on!

This time, though, she was wearing jeans, her favorite hooded UC Davis sweatshirt, and running shoes. Predictable and practical.

But what wasn't so predictable was the denim bag slung across her chest. That wasn't something she owned. Zafira poked around inside and found a flashlight, a full water bottle, and a box of matches.

Hmmm, good Zaffy, that's all pretty handy stuff. Better than a cheese grater and a bike pump. She smiled, thinking back to another dream.

Zafira glanced around a few more times before looking up. The sky was partly cloudy, with the sun peeking from behind a thin cloud. A slight warm breeze ruffled her hair and carried a scent of olives and flowers.

Then a small bird chirped nearby. Zafira turned and saw what looked like a sparrow or a finch. It had a short tail, a small, dark beak, and was a whole mix of colors: brown, black, white, and even some bright blue patches on its head.

Zafira shrugged and was about to head down the dirt path when the bird swooped around her and spoke...or rather, chanted.

It sounded something like: 'Fay-stay-val... Trapt-ar-py... Prof-ay-say.' Over and over, it went: 'Fay-stay-val... Trapt-ar-py... Prof-ay-say.'

Chirp, chant, dive, repeat.

Zafira cocked her head. "Hello, Mr. Bird," she said. "Can I call you that? I don't know if you are a Mr. or Mrs. or Ms. even, but we'll just go with Mr. for now. Is that okay? Sorry, I don't know what you're saying, but maybe you could show me the way to Athens?"

The bird swooped in a gentle arc and turned to the left.

Guess that's a yes.

Zafira accelerated behind it. They trekked through bushy fields, past grid-patterned olive groves, and toward other cropland.

Soon, Zafira saw a man.

He was picking and tossing olives from a cloth under a tree into a basket. He didn't have a shirt and wore baggy, beige shorts.

Well, barely. They looked more like a sheet folded between his legs and belted at his waist. *Almost like a diaper?!*

Zafira figured he probably knew the fastest way to get to Athens. Her dreams were convenient like that. When she called out, though, he didn't turn. She walked closer and tapped his shoulder.

He didn't even flinch.

She poked him harder—nothing. Again—nothing. Then she really went for it, jabbing at the poor man non-stop.

Still nothing?!! By now, she was practically punching him in the kidneys.

Finally, the man stood up, scaring Zafira back a few

steps. But all he did was stretch, rub his neck, and wipe the sweat from his face with a tattered cloth before bending back down to work.

Ohhhh, I get it. It's an invisible dream.

This happened sometimes. There was no real way to know whether the people in her dreams would be able to see and hear her or not. Zafira liked it better when they did, but being invisible was also fun. This time though, she felt let down.

Darn! I had wanted to be a part *of life back here.* Zafira kicked a pebble and grunted. *So now what?*

Mr. Bird kept chirping, chanting, and swooping. "Well, at least you can see me, little buddy." She shrugged and followed the bird toward another group of olive trees.

They came to the end of the grove, crossed a few narrow, rocky paths, and went down another dirt road. Zafira noticed more farmers up ahead. They carried different-sized baskets and containers. The men pushed small carts, and one or two pulled donkeys. There were even a couple of stray dogs barking while dodging feet and wheels.

No one looked up when she passed, and Zafira saluted in exaggeration, knowing full well they couldn't see her. She snorted in disappointment again.

Up ahead, Zafira saw several cramped, off-balance stone huts. They looked like they were attached by dried mud, clay, and...

Maybe even a little spit?

Zafira chuckled to herself, happy to be surrounded by such unusual, old buildings. She twirled around.

No power lines, no cars, no planes, nothing mechanical or technical! LOVE it! Love being back in time!

Something caught her eye off in the distance—high on a

hill. She squinted and shuffled toward it.

An enormous red-and-blue stone palace was surrounded by clusters of bigger and sturdier buildings—both on and below the hill. Next to the palace was a small, narrow structure that looked *kind of* like a Greek temple, but it definitely wasn't the Parthenon.

Zafira frowned.

I planned for the Parthenon, right?

All of a sudden, Mr. Bird zoomed off, squawking and heading right for the base of the hill.

"Wait!" Zafira sprinted after the bird.

She got closer to the hill, where there were more and more people. Zafira wove around a group of sweaty men and noticed many strange outfits. She couldn't help but pause to take it all in.

Most of the women wore colorful, belted, bell-shaped dresses or long toga-like robes. The men mostly wore things that looked like long, belted T-shirts, mid-calf robes, or baggy, folded-up shorts, like the farmer from before.

There were also several soldiers or guards strolling around. Zafira could tell they were soldiers by their protective chest covers and fancy shin guards.

So far, so good. I mean, these people all sorta look like ancient Greeks from movies and books. But... something is wrong with the buildings. They don't look like they should. Plus, where's the Parthenon?!?

Mr. Bird was getting further away, so she went on whizzing past more cramped houses, shaky wagons, and carts full of all types of food. There were bruised cabbages, cucumbers, carrots, and celery; overripe grapes, plums, figs, pears, and dates; and even some gross-looking pork and goat meat. As yucky as it all looked, she liked seeing what type of food was around back then.

Suddenly, Mr. Bird turned. Zafira caught up to the bird and followed it down a narrow, isolated alleyway. Mr. Bird stopped in front of a run-down shack, but it wasn't squawking anymore. Instead, it made sharp, darting movements toward the hut's door.

Does it want me to go in there and be stealthy about it? I'm invisible, so that's easy...

But as she leaned in to eavesdrop on the people talking inside the hut, Zafira heard a hiss from behind her.

CHAPTER 4: SMALL AND TALL

Zafira spun around and screamed—because, yes, you can still be scared in dreams. In front of her was a freaky hybrid creature.

It had the face of a raccoon—with shadowy, black-circled eyes—and the horned, snake-like body and clawed, stumpy legs of a dragon. Its forked tongue darted in and out of its slimy mouth. And the scary *thing* was coming right at her—ready to attack.

It lunged.

Zafira jumped to the side and leaped up onto a short wall. From there, she hoisted herself up onto the hut's low, flat rooftop.

When Zafira planned her dreams, she chose not to make herself stronger or faster or have any special powers because those dreams always ended faster whenever she did. Sure, she sometimes liked being able to fly; once, she was as big as the Hulk. But usually, she stayed regular ol' Zafira. Luckily, that meant being tall and strong for her age, which came in handy now.

She leaned over the edge of the roof. The scary racco-dragon hissed, spat, and glared up at her. It was too short to be able to jump or fly. So, even though it was a dragon, it was luckily more komodo than *Game of Thrones*.

Meanwhile, Mr. Bird, which couldn't do anything to help, just circled and squawked from up above.

Zafira craned her neck to look around. The rooftops were all side-by-side. She could easily jump from one to the other. At some point, though, she'd have to come down, and that creature would surely be waiting.

Nope, not a good idea.

At least, not if she wanted this dream to end before it got going.

Should I throw something at it?

Zafira felt around on the roof—nothing. She looked in the denim bag.

Better not risk breaking the flashlight or losing the water bottle.

That only left the matches, but just the idea of burning down all these old buildings—even if it *was* all make-believe—made her decide against that, too.

The monster kept waiting.

Zafira patted down her clothes and dug into the left pocket of her jeans, where she found the softest, least threatening thing possible: a folded-up, half-empty plastic bag of gummy bears.

Seriously? Gummy bears?

Zafira stared at both the soft treats and the ugly beast below. She shrugged.

Maybe it's hungry or easily distracted?

She flicked a red gummy bear right at it.

The racco-dragon hissed violently. It glared at the treat, but within seconds, curiosity won, and the creature inched forward. After a couple sniffs, it gulped down the gummy with one flick of its tongue.

Zafira saw her chance. She chucked the rest of the gummy bears, one at a time, as far away as she could. The beast, clearly not as intelligent as it was creepy, chased after the treats like they were fetch toys.

Zafira leaned further over the edge and noticed a small window-like opening next to the hut's door. It was her best chance at getting in fast.

Wasting no time, she jumped down. But, before she could hoist herself through the window, the racco-dragon hissed and trampled up behind her.

Zafira screamed and kicked up everything around her: dirt, stones, straw, and even a broken pottery shard to scare it away.

Nothing worked. The thing advanced.

Just then, Zafira noticed a strange spluttering, wheezing noise coming from the creature. Its hissing had turned into…

Coughing?

In seconds, the coughs turned to gags, and then the racco-dragon made choking noises before it appeared to suffocate, falling right in front of her. Zafira prodded it with her foot to check, but it was definitely dead.

The gummy bears must have been poisonous! But why?

Zafira didn't have time to wonder. What mattered was that the creature was dead. And she had killed it—which wasn't such a big deal in an imaginary world—but still, no one wanted to be an actual murderer in their dreams.

Is this going to be both an 'I'm-invisible-AND-the-bad-guy' dream?

She scrunched up her lips and looked up at Mr. Bird. It was jerking its furry head like a hyper chicken toward the shack. Zafira laughed, knowing this was all her own invented story and didn't need to be taken too seriously.

Strangely though, she did feel a pang of…*something*…like when going to the dentist's office. Zafira shrugged it off and faced her feathered friend.

"All right, all right, dude," she whispered. "I'll check it out. Relax."

Zafira peeked in the window. It was a smelly, dark, narrow hut, so it took her eyes a few seconds to adjust to the low light. When they did, her smile disappeared.

In the back corner was a beautiful young girl in a strange, circular wooden cell with floor-to-ceiling planks tied together by thick rope.

The girl wore a muddy, tattered version of the weird poufy dresses Zafira had seen before. It was tight on top, belted, and had red and beige layers in the fluffy skirt. The girl covered her face, but Zafira saw she was wearing the bulkiest, brightest pair of gold earrings she had ever seen on a teenager.

The girl was crying and begging to be set free. Someone laughed somewhere in the darkened hut—a cruel and deliberate laugh.

"Ah, come now, fair one, you must look at me as I continue to enlighten you." Zafira heard a dry, raspy woman's voice. "Yes, lovely Philomela, Princess of Athens, do not hide your beautiful blue eyes from me. Allow me to see the pleasing face that would have charmed and bewitched so many in the future."

Princess of Athens?

"If you wish," the woman continued. "I can return to my own appealing appearance from before? But I prefer disposing of such lies now that we are…better acquainted. Do you not agree, my little birdy?"

The woman cackled as she crept out from the shadows. But Zafira almost fell over when she saw the body connected to the voice.

The creature looked like a huge, human-sized crow—with brown and dark blue feathers and gnarly claws. Instead of a bird's head, though, it had the withered, wrinkly face, neck, and shoulders of an old woman.

The creepy bird-lady—with its knotted, clumpy, dirty hair, tattered feathers, and savage eyes—moved sideways out of the corner. Its clawed feet scratched the dry, hard floor, caked with dirt, brittle straw, fallen feathers, and dirty cloths.

The bird-lady approached the cell, and its slivered lips turned into a horrible, toothless smirk.

"Beautiful Philomela, I know my cage is not as big or as comfortable as the quarters you are used to in the mighty palace on the high citadel. Yet I think it is important for you to experience the sensation of life in a cage, as countless innocent birds do. You princesses keep small birds as pets, no? I believe your favorite is a quail? Delicate, defenseless little creatures, are they not?"

Zafira realized this bird-lady was cruel, mocking the young girl.

The bird-lady went on. "Now, I know all that we have discussed must seem shocking to you, and our time together is almost over, so let us end on a happy subject. Perhaps the glorious festival on the Acropolis?" The bird-lady made a disgusting, throaty, wheezing sound while the young girl stifled a sob.

"It was such a pity you were here, unconscious, and missed it," the bird-lady continued. "I attended, of course, purely as a means to pass the time until you awoke. For you see, Zeus, son of Kronos, insisted that I explain the prophecy—as I have just done—before fulfilling my official duty to carry you away."

Did it say, Zeus? Will Zeus be in this dream? Zafira's mind whirled with excitement.

"At the festival, I spotted your sister, Procne," the bird-lady added. "My, my, she is also quite a splendid young woman. But worry not, my sweet, she cannot rival your magnificence, as the prophecy notes as well. She did look rather sad, though, carrying that ridiculous little basket—so simple, so plain. A meager replacement for the one you were to bring her."

The bird-lady kicked at a destroyed woven basket in the corner before unleashing a horrific noise that Zafira figured was probably laughter. Meanwhile, the young girl kept crying and trembling.

Zafira instantly hated this evil hag.

The horrendous bird-lady scratched its way back to the front of the cage and glared at the young girl before it went on babbling. "Now, now, my dear, you see, by giving me your life, you will stop the prophecy and selflessly protect Procne and Athens. Such is Zeus's will."

Zafira saw the young girl dry heave. She felt so bad for her.

And what's all this talk about a prophecy? I remember Yaya taught me that word just a couple of weeks ago. It's like a prediction... But of what?

The bird-lady kept droning on while pacing in front of the cell. "Oh, but poor Philomela, no one will know about this noble sacrifice because no one will know what might have been and what you did to stop it." The bird-lady creature cackled again.

"No, no! Please!" The young girl barely squeezed out her plea between sobs.

"There, there, Philomela. The time has come," the bird-lady said in a weird sing-song voice, moving its wing between the planks.

The young girl shuffled far against the back corner, took a deep breath, and let out a terrified scream.

CHAPTER 5: CHAOS AND CONFUSION

Zafira was already on the move. She scrambled in through the window and jumped into the dark hut, belting out her battle cry the entire way.

The young girl's eyes bulged when she saw Zafira. "Help me! Please! Help me!!"

Zafira snapped to it. She grabbed the first thing she found — a small vase — and hurled it at the creature. The bird-lady merely swiped it away with one mighty flap of its wings.

"You, stupid girl! Who are you? What is this you try? You cannot hurt me. I am stronger than any mortal man or woman and certainly stronger than a girl. Your interference will now cost you your life!"

Zafira stared at the scary hybrid creature now glaring at her.

It's so gross...and talks so weird...and wait, how can it see me? What should I —

It was too late. The bird-lady struck Zafira down with a single blow.

Its clawed feet were about to scratch Zafira's face when Mr. Bird came yawping and flapping in through the window. Mr. Bird attacked the bird-lady by swooping down and pecking at the wretched woman's eyes.

With that, chaos broke out.

Winded by the fall, Zafira gulped and heaved to get her breath back. The young girl's screams increased to ear-shattering shrieks, and Mr. Bird continued to caw, pounce, and poke at the old woman's head and face.

Meanwhile, the hybrid bird-lady let out a blood-curdling screech and flapped its wings at anything in reach within the tiny hut.

Dust, dirt, and other debris flew all over. It was absolute mayhem.

When Zafira regained her breath, she grabbed one of the bird-lady's wings. The bird creature turned its evil, pruned face toward Zafira, along with its other wing. Right before it struck again, Zafira spat on the old woman's horrible scowl and jumped back.

Okay, it's definitely not going to like that.

Zafira scanned around her in a panic. There was nothing left to attack with!

Out of nowhere, a new noise overpowered the chaos. It was louder than the girl's shrieks and the combined noise of things breaking and shattering. It was even louder than all the squawking.

It was the bird-lady, yelping and wailing.

Zafira, the young girl, and Mr. Bird stared at it.

Within seconds, it was apparent — the bird-lady creature was dying. Its disgusting face bubbled over into melted flesh and open sores. Its wings fell limply beside its body, and when its clawed feet could no longer support it, it fell over to the side. The bird-lady screamed one last scream, gasped one last breath, and lay still.

The hut was silent, and the girls exhaled in unison. Mr. Bird landed on the ledge of the window and peered down at the motionless heap below.

The girl spoke first. "Truly, is it dead? Please, friend, could you check?"

Zafira leaned over the feathered heap and discovered its face had almost completely peeled off. It was gruesome. She covered her eyes with the crook of her elbow and groaned. She had killed a strange hybrid creature for the second time that night.

But at least I saved the princess.

Zafira smiled at the thought.

"It, or she, or whatever, is dead," Zafira said. "I think I killed it. I mean, I guess my spit or something must have burned its face," Zafira then blinked a few times and gaped at the girl. "Hey! You can see me?" Zafira's eyebrows shot up with excitement.

"Of course, I can see you. Why would I not be able to see you?" The girl leaned to the side, looking behind Zafira at the hut's door. "Now, forgive my impatience, but would you please free me from this cage? Quickly?"

Zafira stumbled around, looking for something sharp. She found a small dagger. While she sawed at the rope tie, she wondered how a weird bird-lady with no hands could even use it. Or why the creature didn't use it in the fight.

Or is this just convenient dream placement?

Yaya had once explained that her subconscious put stuff in useful places in her dream so that she could keep going and do what she needed to do.

Within seconds, Zafira pulled open the two planks, and the young girl squeezed out. The girls were finally face to face.

Without a word or delay, the girl grabbed Zafira by the forearm and pulled her toward the hut's door.

"We must leave immediately. That thing mentioned a sister earlier, and I do not want to be here if or when she appears."

They stepped out of the cramped hut and back into the narrow alley. It was now totally dark except for some patches of moonlight. The girl yanked Zafira down the road, and they started to run.

Mr. Bird followed closely.

"Dear friend," the young girl panted. "If you wish to leave and continue on your way, with my deepest gratitude and all my blessings, please go."

They slowed down when they reached a crossroad on the main path. The girl faced Zafira.

"However, I would be honored if you would accept my invitation to my palace, where we can feast and talk in comfort and security. In this way, I could thank you properly for saving my life—whoever you are, and…" she looked at Zafira's clothes and frowned. "Wherever you come from."

Her palace? A feast?

Zafira's interest grew. Her dream was getting back on track. Here was a local girl who could show her what life was like in Classical Greece. Zafira was giddy with enthusiasm, and her answer was obvious.

"I'd *love* to come with you," Zafira replied, trying not to look too eager.

The girl nodded. "Follow me. Stay close." She grabbed Zafira's hand, and off they went again.

The girls turned down one more side street and soon made it out onto the main road. Even in the darkness, Zafira noticed they were going straight up to the top of the hill. It was several hundred feet above the city, and in the moonlight, Zafira saw some rocky cliffs and dark caves on the other side.

The girls scurried up to the top. When they got to a massive stone wall, the princess froze as if she was listening for something and then yanked Zafira into a dark corner, away from the gate.

Zafira ran her hand over the rough stone wall and gazed up at the towering enclosure that soared over thirty feet. "What is this?"

"This is the *pelargikon*. It is the wall that surrounds the citadel. The palace is inside," the princess fidgeted, glancing in every direction.

The princess pursed her lips and exhaled like she was calming herself down. Then she whispered, "We will now enter the gate. I believe there will be quite a disturbance because I have been away—missing—since morning's light." She peeked over her shoulder.

Why does this girl look so nervous?

Zafira squinted into the shadows, afraid another bizarre hybrid monster might be lurking in its depths. There was nothing.

"Further, my father's guards may interrogate you," the princess added. "But do not worry. I will insist that you are treated in the best manner possible, as you are my guest and protector. However, sometimes as a young princess, my wishes are often disregarded..." She frowned. "Regardless, you should now tell me who you are, and then—"

"Wait," Zafira said, interrupting the girl. "I think we should back up and start from the beginning. Who are you, exactly?"

Philomela shushed her. "My name is Princess Philomela," she whispered. "My father is King Pandion of

Athens. The palace above, on the Acropolis, is my home. Certainly, you must already know this if you are here?"

"I'm sorry," Zafira replied in a matching hushed tone. "I'm not from around here, so I don't know about you or your family. Can you tell me some more?"

"Yes. I am daughter to King Pandion and Queen Zeuxippe. My older sister is Princess Procne, who was in a very important festival honoring Athena today. I was to be there as well, and I was tasked to bring her a special basket woven by her own hand. Unfortunately, on my way, I was captured by that harpy and held captive until you appeared and saved me."

"A harpy? Is that what that old bird-lady was?" Zafira leaned against the wall.

"Yes, I believe so. I have never seen one before, although I have been warned by my tutors and elders that they are very dangerous. They are creations of Zeus made to carry people to the underworld. I had been told that they resemble beautiful young women with bird bodies. However, as I witnessed, they can transform into ugly, old, horrible—well, you saw."

Philomela grabbed Zafira's hands and pulled them to the princess's cheek. "Oh, how grateful I am that you saved me from that monster and whatever horrors it had planned."

Zafira smiled while taking her hands back.

A princess? Zeus? A festival for Athena? Mythological creatures?

Her mind buzzed.

This is getting good.

CHAPTER 6: NAMES AND DATES

Zafira noticed the princess staring at her. She must have missed the young girl's question or something.

"I'm sorry. What did you say?"

"Your name. I asked for your name. Please, we must hurry, and yet I must know more about you," the princess pleaded, still whispering.

"My name is Zafira Panos."

"And your age?"

"I'm ten."

"Oh, I am but four summers older. And from where do you hail? Judging by your unusual garments, you must come from lands far away, correct?"

Zafira took a deep breath. This was the part of her dream where she could make up something easy like she was from Zafiraland. Or tell the truth. Zafira wasn't sure yet, so she stalled.

"I come from America."

Philomela squinted and leaned closer. "America?"

Zafira knew Philomela wouldn't know about America

since it wouldn't even be discovered for thousands of years. But Zafira figured if this girl was going to show and tell her all about ancient Greece, it couldn't hurt to share some things from her own time.

But not too much. And she definitely wasn't going to tell Philomela this was all a dream. That never turned out well. In fact, it was usually a one-way ticket to waking up.

So, Zafira decided to make up some crazy time-traveling story.

"And so, I found this door or portal or whatever, and then *poof*—I magically came out in the middle of a field near here. Then I met the bird who took me to you and, well, the rest, you know. And so, this is...Athens, right?"

Philomela nodded in slow motion like she was nudging her brain to work better.

Oh man, she's totally not believing this, and I think I'm losing her.

Meanwhile, Zafira saw Mr. Bird—perched on a small ridge in the stone wall—pivot its neck back and forth between them.

Zafira wanted to distract the young girl, so she zipped on to the next question. "Do you know what the date is, Philo...Philomela, right?"

The princess both nodded and shook her head in obvious confusion. "Date?"

Zafira clasped her hands together like her dad often did in his lectures. "'Date' is like...um...a point in time. Like, do you use a calendar? Do you know what year this is?" Zafira needed to make sure that this was still Classical Greece.

Philomela shook her head over and over, her eyes wide open. "'Calendar?' Well..." she stood up straighter and went on. "Perhaps you are asking about seasons? For this, the stars and the skies tell us all we need to stay organized for festivals, agriculture, and other important events."

"Oh," Zafira replied with mild interest, not getting closer to what she needed.

"Another way we discuss the passage of time is lineage. You see, I know that my father, King Pandion, is the sixth King after The Great Kekrops. My brother Erechtheos, who will be king one day, will be number seven. My grandfather was The Great Erichthonius, son of Hephaestus. He was a very important ruler of Athens."

Zafira squinted at the princess.

Okay, this family history is nice and all...but where's the Parthenon?

She just had to find out.

"So, you call this hill 'the Acropolis,' right?" Zafira asked, sweeping the air around her with her arms.

The princess nodded.

Well, at least that part's right.

"And is 'the Parthenon' in there?" Zafira asked, motioning beyond the wall.

Philomela shrugged. "'Parthenon?' What is that?"

Zafira started to piece it all together. She *hadn't* come to Classical Greece, which was when Yaya had told her they first built the Parthenon.

So, if there's no Parthenon here yet, I guess that means...what? I came back to some earlier time in ancient Greece? Something before the Classical Period?

Looking at the totally foreign yet detailed setting around her, Zafira wondered how she had conjured up all this stuff in a dream if she didn't already know about it.

Then her mind turned to times and dates. But again, her terrible memory wasn't helping much.

What came before Classical Greece?

She thought back to the art history textbook.

I remember ancient Egyptian stuff, but I'm definitely in Athens, and Yaya said that was all B.C.E.

She must have been thinking aloud because Philomela asked, "What is 'B.C.E.'?"

"Um, yeah. So, my grandmother, who's an art historian—that's a person who studies art and history and culture and stuff. Well, she told me that it's the way things get dated. It used to be 'B.C.,' which means 'Before Christ.' But then, not everyone believes in Christ, so they changed it to B.C.E., which means something else. I can't really remember—" Zafira glanced down at the ground.

"Oh yeah! They changed it to 'Before the Common Era,'" Zafira stated. "And that's 'B.C.E.'"

Philomela stared at Zafira with that same blank expression.

"I know, this is all very confusing," Zafira said quickly. "When I first learned it, I was totally confused, too." She twitched her nose and scrunched her lips. "Basically, the important thing to know is that we're supposed to count down to zero when it's B.C.E. and count up when it is C.E., the Common Era, like when I'm from."

Philomela was silent again. Then she murmured, "Before Christ? What is Christ?"

"Oh yeah, whoops…you wouldn't know about Christianity now, would you? Or about other religions and beliefs?" Zafira exhaled before inhaling a huge breath, then explained more. "Well, let's see… I think that's going to be a bit of a longer conversation, and maybe we'll have to do it when we're inside your house—I mean, your palace. The point is since you don't know what the Parthenon is—which will be a very important Greek temple later on—I know I'm in a time *way* before that. I just can't remember when."

But something in the hot, dry, olive-scented air around

her triggered Zafira's memory. "Oh wait! It was 400 B.C.E!"

Zafira's mind went back to that summer trip with Yaya, walking around the Parthenon and talking about how different life would have been twenty-four *hundred* years before—not hours or days, but twenty-four *centuries*!

Zafira did the math and realized her subconscious had mysteriously transported her to a Greek civilization that lived anywhere before 400 B.C.E., when the Parthenon had been built.

Philomela steadied herself against the wall as if all this strange, new information was making her dizzy. Zafira noticed and said, "Anyway, let's get inside, and we can talk more there."

"Yes, I believe that would be best," Philomela whispered. "However, I still know not what to say to the guards about you."

"Oh, well, I don't think you have to worry about that because, except for you and this bird," she said, jerking her thumb up toward Mr. Bird, "I don't think people can see me here. Actually, that's why I was so surprised you *could* see me back in that hut."

"Truly? Is it possible that no one can see you, even though I can without difficulty?"

"We can do a test. Wait here."

Before Philomela could object, Zafira sprinted toward the opening in the massive stone wall.

She ran along with her mom's voice bouncing in her head: 'Zaffy, you never take a second to *look* before you leap!'

But that was one of the best parts of dreaming: leaping first. *And not even looking at all!*

CHAPTER 7: GATES AND GUARDS

The main gate was massive!

It was a wall with a wide entrance that had a mammoth horizontal stone slab on top and two equally huge vertical stone blocks on the sides. Above the top slab were layers and layers of smaller stones, which were stacked in a kind of alternating way so they got closer from both sides as they got higher. They came together to form a triangular point at the top of the arch. A large, carved stone panel was in the middle of this triangle.

It was dark out there, but with the moonlight and some nearby torches, Zafira saw two large columns in the middle of the stone. The columns looked like they were sliced in half and stuck on the front, like decoration. In the middle were two giant carved coiled snakes with their tongues lashing out.

Zafira flinched at the unwelcoming snake doorway. But even more shocking was how the ancient Greeks managed to stack those huge, heavy stones without a forklift or crane.

You'd need a giant to lift those!

Beyond the enormous entrance, Zafira noticed another wall and, to the right, a second entryway. So, it was essentially a backward L-shaped corridor leading inside.

Five guards stood on either side and one on a walkway above the gate. They wore funny-looking pointy helmets with decorative feather things hanging from the top.

Other than that, they were similar to the guards she had seen before, with their short tunics, shiny body armor, and fancy shin guards. They each also carried a spear, and several figure-eight-shaped shields were propped up on a nearby wall.

It was time to test her invisibility. So, Zafira ran out of the shadows and went wild—jumping up and down, yelling the alphabet, and waving her arms around.

If they see me acting crazy like this, I'm sure it'll be straight to the Tower of Death!

She giggled at the thought but felt a little nervous nonetheless. Zafira knew nothing bad could really happen except waking up too soon.

Which would totally suck since there's still so much to see and learn!

Luckily, nothing happened. The guards barely blinked.

Zafira jogged back along the side of the wall until she got to Philomela.

"It's all okay. I'm still totally invisible. We're good to go, and it's a good thing they didn't see me 'cause I was going completely KAH-RAY-zy!"

"KAH-RAY-zy? Zafira, I truly know so few of the words and expressions you use in your speech."

But Zafira knew it didn't matter. Dream people might not get all her idioms, but they at least understood English because—*Well, duh!*—you always dream in your own language.

Philomela looked up toward the top of the wall and spotted a guard getting closer to their shadowy corner. She grabbed Zafira and yanked her down behind a low bush. The girls huddled there for a while.

Zafira didn't say a word. She knew when someone was trying to hide.

When the guard moved away, both girls stood up again.

"Why are we hiding and whispering?" Zafira asked, dusting off her jeans. "Aren't you one of the most important people here? Why don't you want to be seen?"

"Please forgive me for using such force, Zafira. When you left before, I constructed a strategy to remain hidden so that before I am escorted to my parents, I can discuss certain details with Procne...details told to me by that horrible harpy. I thought perhaps you might cause a distraction by the gate, so I could enter without being seen."

Zafira chuckled. "Where I come from, kids usually sneak *out* of a house, not sneak *in*." The princess's brows crinkled in confusion.

Zafira huffed at her joke falling flat. "Never mind. And don't worry, Philomela. Of course, I'll help you."

The girls made their way to the main gate. Zafira noticed Mr. Bird following them, even though it was no longer chanting anything. All of a sudden, her brain made a connection.

"Oh, wait! 'Fay-stay-val,' 'Trapt-ar-py.' 'Prof-ay-say'...I get it now! *Festival. Trapped. Harpy.* Philomela, you were supposed to go to that festival to help your sister, but you were kidnapped and trapped by a harpy! And then, 'Prof-ay-say,' well, that's what that harpy told you about. But I still don't get it. What exactly is all this prophecy stuff?"

Philomela looked down, trembling. "Let us get inside as soon as possible, Zafira. We can discuss everything in detail there."

***

The girls devised a plan as they went. When they got to the main gate, Philomela stopped and crouched down. Zafira kept walking well past the gate until she was in a far-off corner.

The plan was in motion.

First, Zafira picked up some dry shrubs and took out the matches from her bag. Then, going against everything she ever learned from her parents, teachers, and camp counselors, she lit the shrubs on fire and waved the flaming bunch of twigs above her head, hoping to attract the guards' attention.

Zafira wasn't afraid. She knew that even if she *did* burn down the entire Acropolis, it was all just a dream. No harm, no foul, no actual fire.

But since she was already hooked on finding out as much as she could about this princess and this palace, she didn't want it to end. So, she had to be careful.

Within seconds, the guard from the walkway above called out to the others. The men ran toward the fire, leaving only one guarding the main gate.

As the men rushed over, Zafira placed the rapidly burning bundle on the dirt. Zafira saw all eyes were only on the small fire, which again confirmed her invisibility.

It took one guard three or four taps of his foot to extinguish the flame. The group turned back toward the main gate, arguing about what might have started it. Zafira caught the words 'torch' and 'wind' before she jetted away.

Up ahead, Zafira spotted Philomela tip-toeing behind the one remaining gate guard. The guard had eased forward several steps, cupping his ear to get in on his colleague's discussion and missing the princess sneak past him.

Zafira easily entered next, followed by Mr. Bird from up above.

They were finally inside!

The girls made their way across a dark, open area. Zafira wished she could turn on her flashlight to get a really good look. But even with the moonlight and some light from oil lanterns hanging on nearby buildings, she was able to see patches of grass surrounded by pretty flowers and plants.

There were also paths lined with elegant, trimmed bushes and other small trees. Different-sized buildings cast shadows around them, most noticeably a colossal building on the left.

Zafira noticed that everything was very neat and clean.

And it's all so green.

Zafira marveled at how different it was from the modern Acropolis—a much browner and dustier version. Meanwhile, Philomela guided them toward the main building on the left.

"What is that?" Zafira whispered.

"That is the palace," Philomela replied. "Follow me. This, I know how to enter unseen."

The split-leveled palace had a flat roof, a variety of openings as windows, and was five stories tall. Each level was built out of a different type of stacked stone. Even though it was dark, Zafira could see that some stones were smooth and others were rough. As they got closer, Zafira gaped at its size.

It's absolutely gi-normous!

She couldn't understand how the Greeks had built such massive structures.

The girls turned around to the back—or 'north side,' as

Philomela whispered—and Zafira was surprised to see rows of red-and-blue tapered columns. The columns were bigger on top than on the bottom, and Zafira found that very strange.

Their colors were unusual, too. Even at night, the bright reds, blues, yellows, and greens were super bright. Zafira remembered Yaya had told her that—unlike what most people thought—ancient Greece wasn't full of all-white statues and temples. Nevertheless, Zafira couldn't believe *how* colorful it was.

She was still gazing when Philomela nudged her.

The princess pointed up to a large, leafy plane tree.

Before Zafira could ask what she was thinking, Philomela had already climbed into the tree.

Wow! That's one extremely flexible princess!

Philomela kept climbing and ended up on a low ledge at the base of the palace wall. She motioned for Zafira to follow.

"Um...Okay..." Zafira's voice dripped with skepticism.

But even with some doubts, Zafira managed to scramble up to that same ledge. From there, she looked down over the rocky cliffs below. Even though it was all imaginary, she still felt queasy and uncomfortable.

Zafira's anxiety grew when Philomela climbed onto her shoulders, got up to the next level, and dropped a rope the princesses always left hidden. Zafira used it to climb up the side of the wall, making sure not to look down this time.

The two girls balanced their way across from that higher ledge until they reached a short balcony wall. One last easy shuffle over, and they were finally inside the palace.

CHAPTER 8: THE KING AND THE QUEEN

Zafira had barely caught her breath before Philomela was on the move again. The princess guided Zafira into a wide corridor to the left.

Mr. Bird followed along, shadowing their every move from above. Zafira felt comforted having him around.

Halfway down the corridor, Philomela stopped. She flattened herself against an unlit wall. Zafira followed her lead but snickered when she remembered no one could see her anyway.

Two voices came from around the corner. Both girls held their breath and eavesdropped.

"Oh, dear," a woman said, her tone gentle, "I so wish you could have returned sooner to see how lovely Procne was today."

"My parents," Philomela mouthed.

"Yes, my queen," a male voice added. "I arrived as swiftly as possible. I am happy to know my princess was satisfied, as it brings me joy to know you are satisfied, too."

Zafira tip-toed to peer around the corner. She glimpsed

the King and Queen of Athens, who were in a courtyard near the top of a large set of steps leading down.

The king was tall, well-built, and sturdy. He had a crinkly face with a long, pointy beard. He also had short, dark, curly hair and tanned skin. His voice was deep and proud. He wore a mid-calf, colorfully patterned, belted robe. He looked like an ancient Athenian king should: wise and strong, like a super buff professor.

The queen, on the other hand, was willowy; her pale skin was almost iridescent. Golden ringlets fell well below her waist, and shiny bands and pins decorated her hair. She wore a tight-fitting, narrow-waisted gown that bounced into a skirt with beige, cream, and gold layers.

Her head, neck, and arms were layered with gold and ivory jewelry, adding to her gleaming sparkle. Her coiled golden earrings, stacks of brilliant necklaces, and even wide, shiny arm cuffs were so rich and shimmery that Zafira needed sunglasses just to look at her.

The royal couple kept talking, unaware the girls were watching.

"Certainly Procne was so disappointed at first when Philomela did not appear with her special woven basket," Queen Zeuxippe said. "Nevertheless, the procession began, the maidens performed, and we slowly arrived to Athena's monument where the sacrifices were given."

"My king, if only you could have seen that Procne was one of the most beautiful young maidens," she added. "But oh...how upsetting about Philomela. She was seen leaving the citadel late this morning, running in her tardiness. And now, I am certain she is hiding somewhere in shame. When I see that horrible child, I will punish her with my own hand. However, no one has seen her yet today. Do you think we should be worried, my love?"

"No, no, my dear. As you mentioned, she likely only escaped for the day. She will appear. But, we need not think about her at this moment, for there is more urgency in Tereus's offer. He is ready and quite anxious to wed Procne as soon as I give my blessing. We are still agreed about this wedding, are we not?" King Pandion asked his wife.

Zafira turned around and saw Philomela's horrified face. Zafira figured this wedding announcement must be news to her.

"Of course, my king. I did have my reservations about his suitability, in particular physically. Yet, if indeed he has been a great political help, and will continue to be an invaluable military ally, then we must ensue."

"Fine. It is settled." The king cleared his throat. "When do you think we should proceed with the ceremony? I would like to finish this before the great festival this summer. Will that be possible?"

"Yes, of course, my dear. We can prepare everything quickly," the queen said. "However, I must urge you once more. You *are* certain that of all possible suitors in the land, he is the best choice for our eldest?"

"Yes."

"So it shall be. I will begin preparations and tell Procne tomorrow."

As the king and queen went down the stairs, their voices faded. Philomela leaned toward Zafira and whispered, "They are going to the *megaron*—the largest, most central room in the palace. It is where official business and meetings take place. My parents often enjoy passing time there after the sun has set. I think they will not come back this way."

Philomela sighed and continued. "My quarters are at the end of the next corridor. There is a small food storage chamber nearby where we can retrieve something to eat and drink."

The princess looked into the shadowy distance before adding, "Forgive me, Zafira, I know we have much to discuss, but I have now received some unfortunate and upsetting information. I must think on it and then speak with my sister as quickly as possible. Please, follow me to my chamber."

Even in the darkness, Zafira could see Philomela's face was ashen. She felt bad for this girl who—just tonight—had already been kidnapped, almost killed, and now given some bad news. Sure, she wasn't real, and Zafira didn't know her, but something nagged Zafira. So, she followed along, hoping to figure out what.

***

The girls turned down another corridor. This one, though, had more of the massive, bulging, unevenly top-heavy columns Zafira had seen before. Zafira thought they were funky but pleasing in a weird way, too.

The girls made their way around a landing of wide steps and went down yet another colorful, column-lined hallway.

Zafira loved being guided down these long, wide, mysterious corridors. She could hear Theo Leo's voice ringing in her ears: 'It's nice to see how the other side lives!'

It was still dark, but from flickering oil lamps, Zafira glimpsed the decoration around her. There were geometric tile designs on the floor, colorful paintings of oversized animals and nature scenes on the walls, and a checkerboard-decorated ceiling. Plus, every single column or doorway was partially, if not totally, painted. Some were even made of gold or ivory.

Zafira thought about how everything in this time—from

the palace to the clothes to the jewelry—was so over-the-top.

It's like a Beverly Hills heiress's mansion mixed with a Las Vegas casino combined with Buckingham Palace. And all of it sprinkled with gold and glitter!

As Zafira took it all in, Philomela whispered, "Be careful as we get closer to the living quarters. We will surely not see my parents again, but my brothers might be awake and hiding."

"Okay." Zafira heard the sadness in Philomela's voice and felt a pang of compassion for her.

The girls arrived at a doorway leading into a kind of storage/pantry room. Inside were elaborate bowls, painted jugs, and colorful vases of all sizes. They held different types of vegetables, fruit, grains, and even what looked like tiny dried fish. There were herbs in smaller containers, and some oversized painted vases were full of water and a red liquid, which Zafira guessed was wine.

Since it was too dark to see anything, Zafira decided it was safe to finally use her flashlight. She took it out of the bag and switched it on.

Philomela gasped.

"Don't worry, Philomela," Zafira reassured her. "This is only something from my time, like a tool. All it does is give light. It won't hurt you. It'll just help us find food faster."

The princess eyed the strange light source as if it were going to stab her. She then grabbed a handful of thin flat bread and a small bowl of olives. Zafira took some chunkier bread and a few pears from a basket.

Most of the vases and bowls looked like yellow or red clay containers. Zafira remembered Yaya had explained the clay the ancient Greeks used was called terracotta. These containers were painted with fancy designs: nature scenes, animals running, or even pictures of stick people marching in some sort of parade.

Zafira noticed piles of thin, really shiny gold bowls, plates, cups, and other tableware on a nearby table. Some other ones were gleaming silver, and even a few looked like they were made out of ivory.

"It is late now, so this will only be a small meal," Philomela said. "Tomorrow, for breakfast, we will dine on nuts and hearty breads smeared with assorted fruit spreads. Also, Zafira, there is no need to take water, for the servants always leave me a container in my chamber. There, I also have cups and many *rhytons*."

Before Zafira could ask what a 'rhyton' was, they heard steps coming from outside the door.

Zafira fumbled with the switch of the flashlight, dropping her food in the process. Philomela ducked behind an amphora but knocked a nearby table leg. Zafira had to lean over to catch a tall, thin pitcher before it smashed to bits.

A tired, portly woman entered the storage room carrying a candle and a small cup. She froze when she saw the pitcher floating in midair.

But just as she blinked and rubbed her eyes, Zafira put the pitcher right-side up on the table. When the servant looked again, everything was back to normal. She shrugged, filled her cup from a large water amphora in the corner, and left the room.

"That was close, Zafira," Philomela whispered as she crawled out. "But you saved us, indeed!"

Zafira chuckled and glanced away. The girls finished collecting their food and finally made their way to Philomela's room.

CHAPTER 9: DECORATIONS AND DETAILS

Walking through the hot, shadowy, ancient palace, Zafira could barely see anything. But she could tell her strange, new friend felt sad about something.

I wish I could help her. Maybe tell her about my cave time?

Ever since she had been old enough, whenever Zafira was upset about something—like when she didn't get invited to Sarah Jensen's scavenger hunt birthday party when she was eight or when she got her first C on a math test and *especially* when she got into a fight with her ex-best-friend, Megan Hutchinson—Zafira did something Yaya had taught her, which always made her feel better.

Zafira would turn off all the lights in her bedroom, pull down the blinds, *and* draw the curtains to make the room as dark as possible. Then, she would crawl into her bed, surround herself with pillows—by her sides, by her head, by her feet—close her eyes, and picture herself in a dark cave.

She would try to imagine what it smelled, sounded, looked, and even felt like. Along the way, she would cry and cry until she was exhausted and sweaty. Miraculously, at some point, whatever had upset her ended up being sucked away into that darkness.

Afterward, she would turn on the lights, open the window, and feel great. Zafira had always *loved* that feeling of crisp air and bright light.

It was like a fresh start.

She always liked being able to start again, and she had a feeling that might be exactly what Philomela wanted to do, too.

They soon reached the princess's sparsely decorated, almost empty bedroom.

All that gold and decoration but, like, no furniture?

"Please, come inside. You are most welcome." Philomela gestured for Zafira to explore.

The room was a large rectangle, with only a bed, two tables, and a bench—all built-in and attached to the stone walls. The twin-sized bed in the back corner had a small woolen pillow and a few thin blankets folded on top. Along another wall, there was the long, low bench with lots of colorful cushions on it.

Several squat, rectangular, glass-less window holes were up near the ceiling. Zafira recognized that based on where the room was located in the palace, they were near the edge of the cliffs they saw when they climbed up from the tree outside.

In a corner along the other wall, on the two built-in tables, there were lots of baskets, terracotta vases, and storage containers.

In the last corner was a narrow terracotta bathtub next to a pedestal with a large, golden bowl on top. The tub was hidden behind a strange divider that came up about waist-high and had more red-and-blue, top-heavy columns. Several short, cross-legged stools were the only moveable pieces in the room.

Even though the room lacked 'stuff,' it was still fully decorated. Murals filled every inch of the floor, walls, and even ceilings, with designs of bright green trees and plants, multi-colored flowers and birds, bright mosaics, and millions of geometric patterns.

Zafira twirled around, looked up, and took it all in.

Meanwhile, Philomela, silent and engrossed in thought, changed out of her muddy dress into a floor-length, light brown linen nightgown. She also took off her shiny, dangly earrings.

Zafira noticed Philomela placing her earrings in a container full of gold and ivory jewelry.

"I guess you really like gold accessories, right Philomela?"

"Why, of course, Zafira," Philomela replied matter-of-factly. "I am the princess. Gold is an essential part of our lives. As royals, we must be adorned with it as often as possible. Do you not wear gold yourself, Zafira?"

Zafira shook her head, curled her lips in a cringe, and pictured herself showing up to school tomorrow draped in gold jewelry. *Everyone would just* die *laughing!*

Philomela walked over to the table and picked up a pitcher of water and a terracotta cup sculpted and painted like an upside-down octopus. She poured some water and handed it to Zafira. Philomela then got her own cup, which looked like some type of animal head.

"What is this?" Zafira asked, holding on to the cup's curvy tentacles with both hands.

"It is water. Or do you prefer wine? Or a mix?"

Zafira snorted. *Yeah, I doubt mom would like me getting drunk in my dreams!*

"No, water is fine," she replied. "I mean, what is this

type of cup?"

"This is my *rhyton*. *Rhyta* are animal-shaped drinking vessels, usually used for ceremonies but also available for daily use. We have them in gold and silver, but I prefer them in clay because of the lovely details in the painted designs. Truly, you must also have them where you are from, and perhaps in even more elaborate shapes?"

"No, we don't," Zafira said with a little chuckle. "And it's too bad actually...these are great!"

Philomela smiled and took a sip. She stared off into the distance and rubbed the side of her jaw. She seemed to be in pain.

"Are you alright?" Zafira asked.

"Oh," Philomela glanced up and smiled. "Yes, please excuse me. It is only that I have felt some strange pain since this morning...in my mouth, or perhaps it is my tongue? But it is nothing. I must have bit something in a bad manner."

She shrugged before adding, "Zafira, I do hope it will be suitable for you to rest here while I find my sister. May I please offer you one of my night tunics for your sleep?"

Zafira downed the rest of her water and nodded, even though she knew sleep was impossible in dreams.

"Perhaps my guest would also like to bathe?" Philomela asked, leading Zafira to the small terracotta tub. She showed Zafira which water jugs were used for bathing and filled the golden basin with fresh water.

Philomela also motioned toward two smaller basins, which, Zafira realized with mortification, were probably the toilet. The princess finally pointed to another nearby shelf with several thin linen cloths and various oils.

Zafira nodded and smiled. "Thanks, Philomela. But I think I'm okay."

Philomela explained that there were just four 'personal

wash basins' in Athens, and they were only for her parents, her brothers, Procne, and herself. Bathtubs were a luxury reserved for royalty.

"I know how truly privileged I am," she continued, a bit embarrassed. "We also have moving water, for there is a vital water spring up the hill, to the north," Philomela pointed out of one of the windows.

"Our water flows due to the natural decline in the land, from the highest point, which is near the gate we entered, to the lowest point on this side of the palace. We use the basins for our needs, and the servants take them away to the moving water."

"Oh, that's interesting," Zafira said, imagining life without plumbing. She had a long talk once with Yaya, who had explained how the Classical Greeks had some public baths, but it wasn't until much later, with the Romans, that plumbing systems were really developed.

Life without a toilet... That would suck.

Whenever Zafira time-traveled in her dreams, she was happy to experience life in a different period. But then, she was also *really* happy to wake up to her modern conveniences back home.

Zafira changed into the tightest, itchiest nightgown ever. Meanwhile, Philomela brushed her own hair with a small ivory comb and asked Zafira to tell her more about the future.

Zafira dodged the princess's questions, avoiding going into too much detail because she didn't want to waste time in her dream on stuff like that. But she *did* mention how important the ancient Greeks were for history.

"It's because of you guys that we have things like geometry and democracy and stuff," Zafira explained. "My dad is actually a professor of all this, so you see, we even *teach* stuff from your time in our universities in the future."

Philomela beamed.

Zafira kept going. "Athens is a big city in the future, and even the Acropolis is still around with this huge temple called the Parthenon on it. I mean, my grandma told me that it was partially blown up in a war or something, but it still stands, and it's an important monument later on. So, I don't know about all this prophecy stuff you were talking about before, but you should know that Athens will be fine in the future."

Philomela stared down at her comb as if in a trance.

Suddenly, an angry young girl stormed into the room.

"There! Philo! What a little donkey you are!"

And that must be the sister...

CHAPTER 10: DOUBTS AND DECISIONS

Philomela rushed over to her sister. "Procne, dear elder sister, you must forgive me. I am so sorry! You may not believe what happened, but—"

"Stop! Philomela! I cannot bear to hear yet another of your imaginative stories," the young girl said and grumbled. "I am so angry! I looked so foolish with that ridiculous substitute basket. I should have had the best! Am I not the eldest daughter of the King of Athens?"

Princess Procne paced the room, shrugging her shoulders and waving her arms as she ranted. She looked a little like Philomela: both girls had long, wavy hair and lean, slender bodies. But that was where the similarities ended.

Philomela was fair-haired and fair-skinned, like her mother. Her eyes were blue-green, and her features were very proportionate and delicate. Procne, on the other hand, had auburn hair, olive skin, and brown eyes. Plus, her eyebrows, nose, and chin were all slightly unbalanced, and her ears were noticeably too small.

Sure, both girls were beautiful, but Philomela's beauty

was the type that would make everyone turn and stare, look and compare, admire or glare.

However, when Zafira noticed Procne's outfit, Zafira blushed. The other princess had a very colorful, geometrically patterned, tight-waisted bell skirt that flowed down to the ground in wavy layers—like most other dresses Zafira had already seen. But the top part was genuinely shocking.

It was short-sleeved and multi-colored, like the bottom, except the whole middle part was missing. Her small chest poked out of a scooped neckline that fell *below* her breasts instead of below her neck.

Zafira figured it was probably some sort of traditional costume that Procne had to wear for the festival. *But it was so...totally...naked!* On instinct, Zafira crossed her own arms over her chest while Procne fumed.

"Oh, Philomela! I was not even the most beautiful nor the most talented! If only you could have seen the elegant ceremonial gown that Euterpe wore. Or Ligeia's singing. And several maidens performed a special dance together... It was magnificent. And Euterpe wove the most beautiful little red flowers in her golden hair. Indeed, she was so lovely. Philomela, why were you not there? I felt so alone. I could not see mother or anyone!"

Procne plopped down on the bed and started to cry. Philomela sat beside her, put her arm around her, and leaned her sister's head on her shoulders with love and care.

"Please, I beg you to believe me, Procne... I was on my way, bringing your finely-woven basket. I wanted so badly to be there for you. Certainly, I cannot deny that I did sleep too late. But I would have made it, except..."

Procne lifted her head and pierced her sister with a contemptuous, challenging glare.

58

"Except, mistakenly, I chose to pass through the small alleys where father always tells us never to go, and this is where the crime occurred. For you see, once there, I was tricked, trapped, captured, and nearly killed by...by...a harpy!" Philomela burst into tears.

Procne pulled away and scowled at her sister.

Zafira hung back in the corner by the tub, taking in the dramatic exchange between sisters. She felt bad for Philomela, begging for her sister's forgiveness, and wondered why Procne couldn't forgive her sister.

Just let it go already, girl.

Instead, Procne was at it again. "Oh Philo, must you continue to disappoint and ridicule me in this way...with this fantasy? Speak honestly! Tell me you chose sleep over your sister. Or say you did not even want to come. But please, do not create a story you believe I would be stupid enough to accept. It is absurd!"

But Philomela went on, pleading for her sister to believe her. She described the horrible harpy and her wooden cage. She told her how Zeus had sent the harpy to kidnap, torture, and eventually transport her to the underworld because there was a prophecy that said the two sisters would cause great destruction and suffering for Athens and unbelievable grief for their own father, the King of Athens.

"The creature spoke of how we will become more horrible after you get married. It said that in a few years, you and I will change drastically, and the needs of Athens and of our father will be far from our minds," Philomela's voice trembled. "Rather, all we will selfishly consider is revenge against those who will bring us tremendous suffering and harm. It even said that you will be the cruelest of all. But since it is my beauty that will be the root of the evil, Zeus ordered only my destruction. Oh, sister, can you believe it?"

Philomela sobbed openly.

Zafira's eyes bulged. *So, that's what the prophecy's about? These sisters are going to turn all bad and destroy Athens? But that's impossible!*

Zafira was so engrossed that she almost forgot it was all a dream!

There'll be so much to put in my journal. Zafira concealed a smile and listened on.

Procne clearly wasn't buying her sister's story. The older princess put her hands on her hips, tilting her head in an 'are-you-serious' way.

Philomela's face looked stricken and unsure, not knowing what to do next. So, she took a deep breath and blurted out the rest, including how Zafira jumped through the window, fought and killed the harpy, and how they sneaked into the palace.

She ended by telling Procne all about Zafira—how she was invisible and came from the future.

Zafira flinched. That was too much for anyone to believe.

Of course, Procne stared at her sister like she was a monster with five heads.

"Oh Procne, please do not look at me so! You must try to believe me. Further, and now I must say the worst of it… When we first entered the palace, we hid and then overheard mother and father talking. Oh, dear Athena," Philomela said, looking up at the ceiling. "How can I even speak the words?" She closed her eyes for a second, nodding to herself.

Then, she opened her eyes and said, "So, I heard our parents say that you are to marry the wretch Tereus as soon as possible. Can you believe it? What are we to do?"

Philomela collapsed at the foot of her sister's legs,

hugged them, and placed her head sideways in her sister's lap, an act full of despair. The whole thing was so emotional and awkward that Zafira was grateful for her invisibility.

Meanwhile, Mr. Bird seemed to be taking it all in quietly on a ledge by the window.

Procne shook her head. Neither girl spoke or moved for what felt like forever.

Finally, Procne got up and wrenched her legs away from Philomela's embrace. She wiped a lone tear from the corner of her eye and spun around to leave in a dramatic move that Zafira thought was straight out of a soap opera.

Suddenly, though, Procne turned around, and Philomela jumped up. The two sisters were face-to-face. Procne glared at—and almost through—her sister before slapping her.

Hard.

Philomela inhaled sharply, pressing her palm to her cheek.

Procne spun around again, ready to leave, but that was when she saw Zafira. Or rather, she must have glimpsed one of Philomela's nightgowns floating midair. She froze.

"Procne? Can you see her? Can you see Zafira?" Philomela rushed next to her sister.

Procne looked first at her sister, then at the floating garment, then back at her sister, and again at the garment. She mumbled 'phantasma' and fainted on the spot.

Philomela tried to catch her mid-fall, but Procne slid down her side, fell to the floor, and lay still.

Philomela bent down to examine her sister. "She is asleep," she confirmed.

"I don't think she can see me," Zafira said. "I think she only saw your clothes. Just like the guards only saw the shrubs on fire and the servant only saw the water pitcher. People can only see things from here, but not me."

Zafira wondered why Philomela and the bird were different, though. Her invisibility dreams were usually all-or-nothing.

"Truly, she cannot see you, for she believes you are a ghost," the princess replied while re-positioning Procne.

"Zafira, please forgive Procne's anger and disbelief. I have a very turbulent relationship with my sister. She is but one summer older, but sometimes...well, she does care for me deeply, even though she does not display this often. I also love her very much. You see, our palace is spacious, and it can often be too empty for two young girls. In this way, I am happy to have my sister as my friend and companion."

Zafira nodded, even though she couldn't relate to having a sister or living in a huge palace. "So, what do you think we should do?"

"I know exactly what we need to do," Philomela answered with a determined look in her eyes. "We need to see Athena."

CHAPTER 11: GRIPPING AND GRABBING

The plan was to take a sleeping Procne back to her bedroom—in case someone checked in on her—and then go to the temple and shrine dedicated to Athena beside the palace.

"It is where Athena's statue resides. Where we pray and bring offerings during festivals and sacred periods," Philomela explained while changing into a plain, dark brown dress. "Further, it is where we ask our great goddess for help or for things we desire."

Athena's statue! Zafira struggled to contain her excitement.

Philomela tied her hair back with several dark hair bands and a few golden pins. "You see, Athena is mother to us all, and she will not forsake us. We must consult her. We will ask her to stop Procne's wedding, help us get you where you need to go, and protect me from the prophecy." She looked back at Zafira, her eyes pleading. "We must not wait any longer. Please, dear Zafira, forgive me, but I beg you to change immediately."

Zafira put back on her crusty jeans. Philomela grabbed a small woolen sack and snatched things from around her room: a light blue shawl, a tiny linen pouch filled with dried fruit, a small dagger, and a few other things, including a handful of miniature statues that resembled little wooden dolls.

"My prayer figurines," she explained.

Then Philomela turned and called out to Mr. Bird. "You stay here now, little friend. How it would please me to keep you as my favorite, most treasured pet—in gratitude for all you have done for me, especially bringing Zafira to save me. But we can manage on our own now, and it is time you rested."

The girls picked up Procne under each shoulder and left. They tucked the sleeping princess into her own bed before racing back down the columned corridors and through the open courtyards of the palace. Zafira figured Philomela *really* wanted to get to Athena's temple since getting caught didn't seem to faze the anxious princess anymore.

Zafira was amazed at the absolute darkness around her when they reached the terraces outside the palace. Sure, there were patches of moonlight, but a night without electricity was what Zafira imagined the bottom of the ocean would be like: a complete blackout.

Hmmm, I bet an underwater dream would be cool. Zafira made a mental note for a future dream.

Up ahead, a tall, narrow temple became visible through the shadows. "We are nearly there. It is just along the sacred path." Philomela pointed toward a tiny walkway, and the girls marched down single file.

Out of nowhere, something grabbed Zafira by the left ankle and yanked her back. She yelped, and Philomela spun around.

Before Zafira could see what had grabbed her, something else seized her by the left thigh. Two thick strands of something clutched her left arm and right knee. She was being pulled off the path by something with long, thick ropes!

Except these weren't ropes. They were alive!

Slowly but deliberately, the tentacles—or whatever they were—tightened their grip around Zafira's confined limbs. It was too dark to see. She tried to reach over with her right arm to pull away whatever was grabbing her, but the second she touched the thick, sticky strands, they only clenched more.

She tried to free herself, but its grip was cutting off circulation in her leg and ankle. She panicked, full of terror. Of course, the logical part of her brain knew this was a dream. But an emotion like fear was a basic instinct, even in sleep.

"Philomela! Hurry! Can you do something? Can you find something to cut this?"

Philomela took out the pointed dagger from her sack.

As Zafira squinted in the moonlight, she saw the tentacles were thick, leafless vines of some kind—or a weird type of root.

Meanwhile, Philomela sawed away. But nothing she did affected the vines.

"Truly, I cannot understand. The more I try to cut, the tougher the skin of this strange plant becomes."

It was definitely some type of plant, but straight out of Dr. Seuss. It looked grayish-blue, and its root-like vines were half-covered in small, pointy thorns and half-covered in bumps that looked like a cat's tongue. If the thorny side had been facing in, it would have easily sliced through Zafira's limbs by now.

"Is it getting tighter?" Philomela asked while trying to pull away the cords from Zafira's right knee.

"Yes! Now my arm's getting strangled, too. Can you get the matches out of my bag? Maybe we can burn it?"

"Matches?" Philomela asked.

"Yes, matches!" Zafira said, grunting. "They're in a small box. It's the only small box in my bag. Just start looking, and I'll tell you what to do!"

"Ah yes, Zafira...right away. But please, I beg you, try not to move as much. I think the more you struggle, the more it tightens."

Easier said than done!

Zafira realized this would probably be the end of her dream—much too soon.

"Hurry up, Philomela! Please!"

While Philomela rummaged through Zafira's satchel hanging by her hip, Zafira felt her body throb. It was almost *too* real. And suddenly, Zafira was really, really afraid.

The princess finally took out the box of matches and held them in her palm.

"What would you have me do now, Zafira?"

"Just...just take one from inside, and can you feel that..." Zafira gasped for air. "That rough strip on the side of the box?"

"Yes"

"Okay," Zafira gulped. "Take one match and, using the round part on the...on the...on the top, strike it all along the side of that rough strip."

Philomela tried to light it several times...and failed. A few times, she just poked the box with the match and even jabbed at it like a horror villain with a knife.

Zafira screamed with impatience. "Here, Philomela, give...give it to me! Give me a new one...put it in my right hand. And if you ho...hold the box—" Zafira struggled to get the words out. "I can try to light it."

Teamwork worked, and within seconds, Zafira handed Philomela the lit match. But the princess—who had never held a match before—placed her fingers too high up, flinched at the burn, and dropped in on the ground.

Out it went.

Zafira groaned, squirmed, and started to shake. "Hurry, Philomela! It's getting tighter and...and I can't feel my...owww...my foot or hand. Quick...another..." Zafira barely squeezed out those last words.

This time, Philomela knew what to do, and she carefully held the lit match near the vine wrapped around Zafira's left leg. Zafira was sweating and crying. She shrieked with pain. The throbbing was unbearable.

Why is this hurting so much? Maybe I should just wake myself up?

The match blackened part of the vines, but they kept crushing Zafira. "I cannot believe it. This strange plant is unaffected by fire!" Philomela screamed.

"Please! Please! Help me. I can't...I need..." Zafira cried in agony, barely glimpsing Philomela's horrified and helpless stare.

Okay, that's it. It was fun while it lasted. Wake up, Zafira. Wake up, Zafira. Wake up!!

Usually, that was all it took to snap out of her dream.

And yet, she was still there while Philomela was panicking.

"Oh Zafira, you saved me, and here I am, doing nothing. What can I do? Shall I retrieve help?"

Zafira pulled her closer.

Philomela cradled Zafira's head and cried, staring into Zafira's tortured, nauseated face and squirming at the sight of Zafira's pale and lifeless limbs.

Foam started to ooze out of Zafira's mouth.

Philomela gaped at the spit trickling out.

"Your saliva!" Philomela said and shrieked. "It worked on the harpy, so perhaps—" She took out her blue shawl, wiped some of Zafira's spit, and spread it all over the plant.

Miraculously, the plant burned and bubbled as if the spit was acid.

Zafira tried to come up with as much saliva for Philomela to sponge up as possible. Soon, the plant withered, and Philomela managed to untangle Zafira from its vice-like limbs.

Zafira was cut and scratched, but at least she was loose.

She whimpered and jerked—still in pain. And her mind was fuzzy. Zafira had never *not* woken up before. Something really weird was going on. First, she dreamed of a place she didn't even know, way earlier than the time she actually wanted to visit. Then, all these strange events happened. And now this—feeling all that pain like it was real and not waking up.

I've got to snap out of this and get out of here. I've seen enough this time. Yup, good enough. Time to go. Come on, Zaffy. TIME. TO. GO!

CHAPTER 12: ATHENA AND THE GIRLS

Zafira still didn't wake up. She was lying on the path in ancient Greece.

I mean, I know I'd asked for adventure and excitement, but this is a bit much.

All of a sudden, all she wanted was safety and boredom. She got up, wobbly and woozy. It was just all *too* real.

"Zafira, please, perhaps you should rest more?"

"No, I'm okay," Zafira replied, wondering if she needed to get away from Philomela to wake herself up.

Yaya told me about all that subconscious stuff, so maybe I still want to help her deep down? But actually, all I want to do is ditch her and all this craziness.

Philomela helped Zafira find her balance. "Are you certain, friend? Dawn is near, but it is still night. We could sit here some more?"

Zafira rubbed her arms and legs. "I'm fine, really. And I was thinking…" *I need to get away from you!*

But Philomela seemed to have her own agenda. "Yes, you're right. You can rest inside the temple. Follow me, and please, stay close."

Zafira sighed and figured she might as well keep up. She could always leave after seeing the temple. Plus, there was still a chance she could see the giant Athena statue Yaya had told her about. So, she trailed behind the princess—this time using her flashlight to check that the path was safe and clear.

The Athena temple definitely didn't look anything like the Parthenon. First, it was very narrow and tall—nothing like the squat rectangular shape of the more modern version. Second, its front, or 'faa-saad' as Yaya taught her to pronounce façade, was made out of wood and stone— nothing like the marble structure she had seen. And finally, its roof and walls looked more house-like than a temple.

The entrance had three doorways, with two large columns between each door. Like the palace, these columns were red-and-blue and seemed bigger on top than on the bottom. There were also small, colorful geometric patterns on the edge of the roof and all along the sides of the temple. But these decorations were less flashy than the ones in the palace.

Zafira looked higher and noticed a row of oversized windows with large crisscrossing slats. Then she looked down, and something strange caught her eye. She shined the light down on a red, round puddle of what looked like— and, unfortunately, smelled like—dried blood.

"What is that?" Zafira asked, repulsed.

"That is the blood remains from the sacrifice yesterday— from the festival for Athena. After the procession, there are performances, offerings, and animal sacrifices. Do you not do the same when you honor your gods?" Philomela asked, her face full of wonder.

Zafira could only grimace a bit and shake her head. She figured now wasn't the time to get into PETA or the future of animal protection.

Philomela went on explaining as they made their way up the steps. "You see, for us, it is an essential part of honoring our gods—which, in my family's case, are also our ancestors. Do you remember when I told you my grandfather was born of Hephaestus, who was a child of Hera and Zeus? Hephaestus was his father, but his mother was supposed to have been Athena. Yet, in actuality, Hephaestus's seed landed on the Earth—known as Gaia—and from there, my grandfather was born."

"Wait, what?" Zafira stopped short. "Are you saying that your grandfather was technically Zeus's grandson? So, that would make you, like, a great-great-granddaughter to Zeus?"

"Yes, it is so. The Athenian royal lineage is full of such things. For example, the city's first leader was an earthborn demi-god named Kekrops—who had the body of a man but the legs of a serpent. After him, the leaders were Erysichthon, Kranaos, Amphyictyon—who was also possibly linked to the demi-god Deucalion—then my grandfather Erichthonios, and now Pandion, my father. Most of them have direct or semi-direct connections to gods or titans, known as the original giants."

Zafira couldn't keep up with all the names, especially such unusual names. But one thing was for sure, this princess was talking about her relatives as gods...being *actual* gods.

I just always thought myths were like ancient fairy tales... Kind of like the Greek version of Cinderella.

Zafira was shocked to realize that this would make Philomela a semi-semi-goddess or quarter-goddess.

As they entered one of the three front doors, Philomela kept talking. "This is the *pronaos*, which is the front section of the temple. Our temple is significant because our gods are very important to us. We know they were born from Gaia and Uranos—the Earth and the Sky. Then, there is a lineage of titans that eventually leads to Zeus. And Zeus, of course, is the father of many other important gods, such as Apollo and Artemis, Hermes, Dionysus, Aphrodite, Ares, and, of course, our own city's patron goddess: Athena, Goddess of Wisdom and Warfare."

Zafira marveled at what she saw and all that Philomela explained. As they went further in, beyond the narrow entranceway, Zafira spotted other colorful columns and smooth stone walls and floors. The floor was also—*surprise, surprise*—colorful and patterned. But the walls were plain, except for several small decorative bands along the top. The ceiling was flat and made of wood.

When Zafira looked up, she noticed an open, smaller second story with more crosshatched windows on all sides. Zafira figured that was so more light could shine on what stood right in the middle of the temple—a massive wooden statue of Athena.

At first, Zafira felt a bit disappointed. It definitely wasn't forty feet tall or made out of gold and ivory—like the one Yaya had told her about. But it was still big and scary, and Zafira was impressed anyway.

"Wow! That's some statue," Zafira exclaimed.

Philomela smiled. "It pleases me to know that our monuments can bring forth such a reaction from those in the future. This, of course, is my favorite one because I have always found comfort in Athena. She is the greatest goddess and a fierce warrior. Surely, she will protect and guide us."

The carved statue was rich with detail, which Zafira couldn't believe these ancient Greeks made using only simple tools. The goddess was stiff, serious, and stared intently across the temple.

She wore a dress that resembled Procne's from before—narrow-waisted, bell-shaped, multi-layered, and, yes, her breasts were sticking out, too. She carried a spear in her long, upraised arm and a shield in the other. On her head, the statue had a huge, elaborate helmet. The whole look screamed: 'I'm a warrior woman. Don't mess with me!'

As if that weren't intimidating enough, behind her feet was a coiled snake made out of wood, which reminded Zafira of the snakes on the main gate. Since Philomela had also just mentioned a serpent, Zafira wondered if snakes were the ancient Athenian mascot.

"Athena is one of my favorite goddesses, too," Zafira said, circling the tall statue. "I've always loved that she wasn't special because she was beautiful but because she was tough and a warrior, too. That's cool. It shows that girls are just as strong as boys."

Philomela took out her wooden figurines and lined them on the base of the statue like devout chess pieces. "Yes, Athena is a great champion and essential in my life. Yet, I do not understand what you say about girls and boys. We all know that boys are the strong, powerful ones."

Zafira scoffed, but Philomela continued. "Perhaps it will be different in the future, but here, women are defenseless and reliant on the men in their lives. Even I, Zafira, with my royal luxuries and privileges as a princess—I am still, first and foremost, a girl, and someday, I will be a woman. This means I am, and will always be, associated with a man. First, that is my father, and one day, that will be my husband. And, indeed, the most important job in my life, as in all women's lives, will be to be a wife and mother someday."

Zafira tried to hide her scowl. She knew enough from what Yaya had taught her that women in the past didn't always have the same rights she had.

"Certainly, women are not to be secluded and hidden away," Philomela added. "We do have some freedoms, but not as many as men. Even goddesses sometimes are not as powerful as gods, and the most significant demi-gods are male. Yet, this is natural. We are all raised with this knowledge."

Zafira would have liked to tell Philomela that things do change in the future, but she understood that it wouldn't help Philomela and might only confuse things even more. Plus, she remembered Yaya taught her it wasn't about being *better* or *worse*. Art historians were always careful not to compare or judge things like that.

Philomela placed her last figurine down and turned back to Zafira. "Also, if a woman does hope to obtain any small measure of privilege, that woman needs to wed. As soon as a woman enters womanhood—erm, you do understand what that is?" Philomela leaned in to whisper the last part.

Zafira grinned. She had grown up with a mom who was a nurse, a liberal grandmother, and her Theo Leo, who loved to tell dirty jokes. She definitely knew *all* about the birds and the bees.

"Sure, like when you get your period and stuff? I mean, I haven't yet, but I know some girls who have."

Philomela blushed and looked away. By her embarrassed reaction, Zafira could tell the princess wasn't used to being so open about the subject. She cleared her throat and continued.

"So…erm…indeed, from that point on, a young girl is expected to marry. A suitor is chosen by her parents. Then, there is a ceremony, usually held in the winter. That season is known as the *gamelion*. The ceremony, which includes a feast and music, occurs in the bride's house. Afterward, the bride leaves her family home to follow her groom to his home. There is often a procession when wedding hymns are sung for the couple."

A husband chosen by your mom and dad?

Sure, Zafira knew arranged marriages still existed in the future, but the idea that her parents could be the ones to choose her husband made her cringe.

Man, they'd probably pick lame Robert Kline from down the street.

"Philomela, what about love? Isn't that important here?"

Philomela shrugged and replied directly, "No. Not for marriages, especially royal ones."

"Oh," Zafira frowned.

"Now, Zafira, please forgive me. The light of day is almost upon us. Soon, the temple will be crowded with worshippers seeking guidance and counsel from Athena. I will begin my prayers now, but perhaps, if you would like, you may rest on the wall by the entry?" She pointed back toward the front.

Zafira knew she didn't rest in her dreams. But she played along so that Philomela could have her prayer time.

But then, that's it. I'll say goodbye and wake up!

As Zafira walked away, she saw Philomela kneel down, holding on to a figurine while gazing up at Athena with eager devotion. The princess then clutched her clasped hands to her chest and bent forward in prayer.

Zafira turned back and found a nice spot to sit down.

Even though she was scared enough to want to wake up, she couldn't help but feel a little satisfied with all that she had seen, learned, and experienced.

I mean, I got to hang out with an Athenian princess! That'll look so good in the journal!

Minutes later, Zafira was still trying to organize all the details for her notes when Philomela joined her on the temple floor. Zafira turned to the princess, thinking of how to say goodbye.

Just then, the ground started to move.

CHAPTER 13: SHAKING AND QUAKING

"What is that?" Philomela exclaimed.

The Californian in Zafira instantly recognized the tell-tale signs of an earthquake. "It's just a quake—an earthquake. Not a big one. In fact—" But then a much stronger aftershock rocked the temple floor. The vibrations jolted every wall, and the wooden beams quivered.

The quake got even stronger with back-to-back tremors that shook everything. Some of the stones in the walls cracked, and little pieces fell. Soon, entire chunks came down, including one large piece above the seated girls.

Zafira looked up just in time. "Watch out!" She pushed Philomela to the left while sliding to the right. The heavy stone smashed to bits right between them.

"We have to get out of here!" Zafira yelled.

All of a sudden, one of the interior columns separating the entryway from the main chamber came shattering down a few feet in front of them. They both stopped short.

The room was full of dust and debris. Both girls were coughing and waving away the powdery air. Zafira caught a glimpse of Athena's wooden face through the dusty shadows. The statue had fallen face first and smashed the column.

"What is—" But Philomela couldn't finish. Part of the central roof in the back bent and cracked, sending beams of wood crashing to the temple floor.

The girls bolted.

They scrambled over smashed stones and fallen wood and made it to the front door. Thankfully, nothing was blocking it from the outside. They got out and ran down to the end of the path.

The Acropolis was full of people running and shouting, so Zafira and Philomela blended easily into the chaos. They zigzagged and hurdled over fallen obstacles. They only hid when they reached a large oak tree—near the main gateway. Both girls coughed and spit. They shared some water from Zafira's water bottle.

They peeked out from behind the tree when they had calmed down and caught their breath. With the early light of day, the ruins were evident.

Some of the palace's rooftops and walls had caved in or fallen down completely. A few other buildings had been partially destroyed. There was a fire burning somewhere in the eastern part of the citadel. Cypress trees had been uprooted, and massive stones were strewn about. Smoke, dust, and rubble blanketed the whole city.

"That building there...why, it used to be a granary," Philomela pointed to a square structure, which now only had three standing walls. "And that...there in the distance," she gestured, "was one of the main storerooms. But now, it...it no longer has a roof!"

Philomela continued to stare and point, her face full of shock. "This is terrible," she cried out. "What has happened to my city? What about my family? My sister? My brothers? Are they safe?"

As if on cue, several guards ran out of a building across from the oak tree. It looked like a guardhouse. They heard one of the guards screaming out orders to several others.

"Pass along this information to your subordinates. The royal family is unharmed, except for Princess Philomela. She has not been seen since yesterday morning," the guard said.

He looked around in alarm and continued. "We do not know if she was even in the palace or on the Acropolis during the quake. The king orders ten guards to search for her—here and outside the citadel. Twenty are to report to the palace for damage assessment, ten more to the temple, and twenty more are to begin a systematic evaluation of all other injuries and damage. We will need to check the caves below the eastern and southern cliffs of the city, as well. Let us begin, men, for it will be a long and difficult day!"

"Oh! What relief! My family is unharmed!" Philomela said, sighing and trembling. "Yet, I am so afraid. I still feel the ground pulsing. What if the shaking returns? What if it never ceases?" The princess broke down into tears.

Zafira didn't know what to do. She wasn't the best at comforting people, even her best friend Vivian, who seemed to cry at *everything*. But she felt awful for this girl, who had already had a horrible day.

Sure, Zafira still just wanted to drop it and wake up. But she knew much more about earthquakes, so maybe it wouldn't hurt to just help her a little more?

Zafira bent down and rubbed Philomela's back. She explained some stuff from science class, including shifting plates, seismometers, and the Richter scale. She was impressed with herself and how much she remembered. Philomela was obviously confused but calmed down a little.

"And don't worry, Philomela," Zafira concluded. "Earthquakes always stop, eventually. There might be some smaller aftershocks, like mini-quakes, for days or weeks after. But you won't feel those. Things will go back to normal, I promise."

Philomela managed a closed-mouth smile and stared out at all the destruction. Meanwhile, Zafira rubbed her own arms and legs, which were sore from before. She felt like she had been through war, and with all the damage, fire, and smoke, Athens looked like that, too.

Bet dad would find this interesting, especially since he's always saying ancient Sparta was the violent, bloody place—not Athens!

The girls suddenly heard chirping from above.

Mr. Bird!

It flew down and perched on one of the branches.

"Oh look, he came to check on us," Zafira said and waved awkwardly. "Don't worry, Mr. Bird. We survived!"

Philomela squeezed out a confused smile. She didn't say anything at first. But then, while still staring at the crumbling buildings in the distance, she said, "Zafira, this is the work of Zeus." Her voice was just a whisper. "He is angry. Only he can make the ground move like so. And only he would dare anger Athena by damaging her likeness. I believe this is a sign." Tears trickled down her cheeks.

"Indeed, I believe the harpy was correct," the princess continued. "The prophecy is in motion! The creature, the earthquake, even the wicked plant—all were meant for me. Do you not see? Zeus *is* trying to kill me!"

"But why?" Zafira asked. She moved closer to Philomela. "What's really going on? I mean, you can't actually believe all this prophecy stuff, right?"

Philomela paced behind the tree. "At first, I did not

believe it. But now...look!" Philomela gestured all around them. "Behold what has already happened to Athens. Look at everything we have endured in just one day! We are being attacked and punished. And I am certain that Zeus, my own ancestor, will not cease until his command is complete!"

Philomela fell to her knees, sobbing.

Zafira hesitated briefly but then kneeled down and hugged her from the side. "Oh, Philomela, come on, prophecies aren't real. Don't cry. It's impossible."

"Listen," Zafira went on, turning Philomela's face toward her. "If Zeus wanted to kill you because he wanted to stop you from bringing destruction to the city, then why would he destroy the city first? I mean, you said that he was the only god who can make earthquakes. So, why would he destroy a city to destroy a girl who *might* destroy the city in the future? I'm not a genius or anything, Philomela, but that just doesn't make sense!"

Philomela's sobs eased off a little. "What you say is true. Why he would do this, I do know not." She sniffled.

"It's all scientific, Philomela. Trust me. You don't know about all this stuff yet, but there've been earthquakes all over the world since the beginning of time. And trust me, the world is a *big* place. You don't know how big yet either, but it's enormous! And these quakes also happen in places where people believe in completely different gods. So, they can't all be because of Zeus."

Philomela had stopped crying, but her eyes were wild with fear. "No, Zafira, these things happened because of Zeus. Perhaps he overheard my prayers to Athena and struck before my beloved goddess could guide me. Surely, I know that Athena is not involved in any way. She has always protected me. Zeus may be more powerful, but she will be so angry about this destruction of her city and her temple. I must not stay to cause a battle between the gods. No, indeed, this has helped me decide what to do."

"What are you going to do?" Zafira asked, not liking Philomela's new decisive tone.

Philomela took a deep breath, steadied herself, and stood up. "My first instinct was to hurry to these guards and show myself. I do not want my family to worry any more than they have. Have I not caused them enough disappointment since yesterday?"

The princess took a deep breath. "However, I am now certain...to protect them all, I must escape. Disappear right now amidst the chaos and confusion. I shall fight my every urge to return to their loving and protective embrace. No, I must not even say farewell."

Zafira's eyes gradually widened. *I don't like the way this sounds...*

Philomela continued. "Perhaps they will think I was killed by this unbelievable occurrence. Perhaps that would be better. They will mourn, and soon after, they will move on." Her gaze was fixed on the horizon, and she rubbed at her chin for a few seconds before continuing.

"Further, my death would surely delay any wedding, which would also help my sister. Maybe in time, my father will recognize that Tereus is not the right husband for Procne. Yes, Zafira, I see it clearly. This has to be the way! I will not stay and destroy everything. I will leave and *save* everything. Right now...with you! Together!"

"So, what are you saying?" Zafira asked with concern, knowing what was coming.

"My dear, Zafira, could I try to go to where you are from? I could help you find your portal and then leave with you?"

Before Zafira could object to Philomela's overly polite

requests, Mr. Bird squawked like crazy and dove between them.

Both girls looked up and peered around the tree to see two guards approaching them.

"Zafira, we must move, or we will be found!"

But it was too late. One of the guards yelled, "Look! There!"

Philomela and Zafira held their breath. The guard was pointing right at them!

CHAPTER 14: WALKING AND TALKING

In reality, the guard's finger was leveled up, pointing at something *behind* them. The girls whipped around and saw a giant falcon, which swooped up the side of the hill and hovered beside the enormous oak tree.

The seriously oversized bird of prey had a gigantic hooked beak, black eyes, and claws like curved daggers. It must have found its mark because it flew straight at the guards. They ran, screaming, toward the guardhouse.

The falcon, which was over eight feet long, didn't give up. It terrorized every guard in the area, sending them scrambling into the shelter.

The last three remaining guards at the gate stood petrified. Still, they stood their ground as if they were bound to protect it, even from colossal creatures.

A bloody battle ensued. The guards tried to throw their spears at the bird, but the bird weaved effortlessly around them. The falcon repeatedly attacked with its claws and its beak. It slashed and killed the guard atop the wall and wounded one more on the ground. The final guard bravely attacked with a small bronze sword, and the two tussled fiercely.

The struggle took both creature and man further inside the citadel, even past the second gate. It seemed like the soldier was trying to get the bird closer to the guardhouse and reinforcements.

Philomela and Zafira watched the horrific scene unfolding before them until Zafira snapped out of it.

"Philomela! Run! It's our only chance!"

The girls sprinted from behind the huge tree trunk and made for the gate. They didn't hear anyone call out or try to stop them. The soldiers were all too busy trying to defeat the mighty winged beast.

It took less than a couple minutes for the girls to get outside the walled city and down the same path they had run up just the night before.

Mr. Bird flew on behind them.

They only paused when they reached some cover—between several large, overgrown laurel bushes.

"What was that?" Philomela asked, panting.

"It looked like a falcon on steroids," Zafira answered. She plopped down, rubbing her sore leg. "What's up with all these crazy creatures? And all these birds? Some are good," she pointed to Mr. Bird, "but most are scary!"

"Do you believe that creature was sent to help or harm us?" Philomela was still gazing back up toward the Acropolis.

Zafira bit her lip when she saw all the sadness and worry on Philomela's face.

"Well, it didn't look like it was after us at all," Zafira said. "If anything, I think it actually helped us get away."

"Indeed, it was quite possibly the only way we could have escaped," Philomela said, puzzled.

"Well, if Zeus is trying to kill you, he probably didn't send it. So, who'd send a bird like that to help us?" Zafira gulped some water from the almost-empty bottle.

"Perhaps it was Athena responding to my prayers?"

A piercing squawk sounded above them, and they gazed up. The falcon flew away, even though its wing appeared slightly injured. They watched the massive bird until it was a black speck on the horizon.

"Well, whoever sent that bird, they'll be happy to know that it's safe," Zafira said.

Philomela nodded and plopped down next to Zafira. They both sat silently for a long spell—hidden behind the laurel bush.

After a while, the girls decided to get up and start walking away from the base of the hill. Zafira kept chanting to herself to wake up. But nothing happened.

I think I can't wake up as long as I'm with Philomela. I have to get away from her, and she needs to just go back to her family.

By now, the girls had passed something Philomela explained was called the outer circuit wall and continued through the outskirts of Athens.

Philomela removed all her jewelry, tied her hair back, and left two long, wavy wisps. These—along with the dirt she rubbed on her face—helped to hide her enough so that when they passed an occasional farmer or other workers, she wasn't recognized at all.

While they were in between a group of trees, Philomela suddenly screamed.

Zafira spun around and saw the tail end of a snake slithering off between the trees. Philomela stood motionless.

"Did it bite you? Are you okay?" Zafira rushed over.

"No...yes." Philomela shook her head. "That is, I am fine. Please forgive my reaction, Zafira. It is merely that I am terrified of snakes. I should not be since they are symbolic to Athenians. But I cannot help it. It did not come near me; only the vision was enough to scare me."

Zafira exhaled. "Don't worry, Philomela. I'm super scared of spiders. And not just the big, hairy ones, but even the small, fast ones." She shuddered.

The girls headed out, following the bird away from the Acropolis. The snake sighting got them talking. First, they told each other about the things that scare them. For Philomela, it was strange noises in the dark, fire, ship voyages, and vomiting. For Zafira, it was riptides, thunderstorms, and wooden rollercoasters.

That led to a discussion on things that were gross: fish that was too slippery to eat and rotting food—for Philomela; stepping on mashed-up banana peels and people picking their noses in their cars—for Zafira.

Onward they hiked over hills dotted with poplar, elm, and olive trees and through fields full of myrtle, laurel, and oleander plants. The early morning sun was heating up, but the girls kept walking and talking.

Zafira didn't know where they were going or what was happening, but she kept playing along, hoping to remember all this for her journal.

Philomela described her family. She told Zafira all about her mischievous brothers, her overly dramatic, often bad-tempered sister, her gentle mother, and her tenacious father.

"I do love all of them very much, and I hate worrying them so." She cleared her throat. "Or disappointing them," she added in a whisper.

Zafira nodded and told Philomela a little about her family: her parents, her uncle, and, of course, lots about Yaya. Zafira explained that Yaya was the one who had taught her about things like aromatherapy and feng shui.

And how to make a crêpe. And where ancient Mesopotamia was. And how to tie a scarf in a million different ways. And how to play Billy Joel's *Just the Way You Are* on her upright piano.

Zafira knew none of this made sense to the princess, but it made her feel better remembering her real world.

"My Yaya always told me to be original and have inner strength. And she says things like, 'There's no 'U' in strength, but there's strength in you.'" Zafira smiled and felt a pang of homesickness, which was unexpected in a dream.

Suddenly, she wanted to wake up in her room, see her parents, and hug her Yaya. Being caught up in an exotic, faraway mystery didn't seem so cool anymore.

Why can't I just wake up already?

Zafira was lost in thought and didn't hear Philomela's question.

"I'm sorry, what was that, Philomela?"

"I asked about your favorite toys, Zafira. I would love to know what you play with in the future."

Zafira told her she didn't play with toys or dolls that much anymore, but she had loved Legos, coloring books, and all kinds of stuffed animals when she was younger.

"I still like to play board games and stuff with my parents. They're both really competitive!" She giggled and explained what all those games and toys were. "How about you, Philomela? What do you like doing when you don't have to do princess things? When you can do what you want to do?"

"I enjoy weaving and practicing my dancing and singing. Further, I am always pleased when I can play alone—with my dolls, wooden toys, or my favorite pet quail."

"A quail? That's your pet?"

"Yes, but Zopy is different. He is a wonderful friend and a loyal companion."

"Zopy?"

"Yes, Zopyros. How unfortunate that we were so rushed in the palace, and I could not show him to you."

A pet quail! I mean, seriously... How am I coming up with this stuff?

Zafira pursed her lips to stifle her laugh.

Philomela meanwhile picked up a wildflower and twirled it. "I also often play games with my siblings," she continued. "We play a game called *astragaloi* where we toss small wooden pieces to each other, which we can only catch here," Philomela used the wildflower to touch the back of her hand.

"We keep all the pieces on our hand as the game continues, which becomes quite challenging. If we drop a piece, we may try to retrieve it, but we must keep all the pieces on our hands—for the winner is the one with the most pieces after three tosses each." Philomela giggled innocently. "Oh, it is so lovely!"

Zafira nodded with genuine interest, and Philomela went on. "Another one of my favorite activities is pomegranate carving. My brother Butes is a marvelous carver. He once carved an entire fish in a pomegranate! It was so true to life!"

"Pomegranate carving?" Zafira laughed.

And so it went. The girls walked and talked. They talked about their favorite food, which included grilled fish, asparagus, artichokes, figs, walnuts, and almonds—for Philomela. And for Zafira, it was her mom's quiche, Orange Chicken, Yaya's spanakopita, pizza, and basically anything with chocolate or, even better, Nutella!

After talking about food, Philomela described other

parts of her life, including palace life. She explained that she didn't have to do any chores but had always secretly wanted to try some. Zafira chuckled at that and told her she wasn't missing much.

Their conversation then turned to singing and dancing, and Zafira made Philomela laugh by telling her she couldn't even make it on to her school choir—even though the kids only had to sing *Happy Birthday*.

"I guess someone has to be *really* bad to mess up *Happy Birthday*," Zafira said, giving a little performance, precisely what had made Philomela laugh.

Philomela explained how much she loved singing and dancing and how they would often watch musical performances in the palace, either during wine festivals or after theatrical dramas. She said her favorites were the wonderful lyre and traditional horn concerts. Philomela told Zafira that a lyre was a popular string instrument resembling a mini-harp.

Even though the day was becoming hotter and hotter, and Zafira was still confused about everything, she couldn't deny it—she was having fun.

But when she looked up, she saw Philomela staring off in the distance, her face full of disbelief. They had been walking up a small hill, and when Zafira got to the top, she gasped at the vast blue horizon.

"Is that...water?" Zafira asked.

Philomela nodded while scrunching up her lips. "Yes. That is the sea."

CHAPTER 15: FLYING AWAY AND RUNNING HOME

Philomela sighed. "My suspicions were correct...that we were walking toward the bay. I have come to the sea with my family many times. Is this near where your portal was yesterday?"

Zafira knew the time had come to put an end to all this aimless wandering. But just as she opened her mouth, Mr. Bird swooped and squawked.

It flittered, tweeted, and chirped for a few seconds more. Then after pausing and twitching a glance at each of them, it darted away.

"Wait!" Both girls shouted, chasing after him. But he flew too fast. Within minutes, Mr. Bird had deserted them.

Philomela burst into tears. "This is ridiculous!" Her breathing staggered. "Zafira, we are *alone*. We cannot deny it anymore. There is nobody. *No body*! No people. Have you not noticed? During our trek, we only passed a few isolated goats! It is as if we are unwanted, unneeded. And now…even our bird friend has left us!"

Philomela raised her arms over her head, lifting her sorrows to her gods. Meanwhile, Zafira nibbled at the cuticle on her thumb and furrowed her brows at the princess.

Philomela paced again. "You see, I am starting to understand that I am not meant to go with you. Of course, it was foolish of me to think I could travel to the future!"

Zafira sighed with relief while Philomela kept going.

"Perhaps I am fated to be bad luck for everyone in my life. I should stay away from those I love, for I only bring disappointment and pain. If I return home, the prophecy is sure to come true. That would be horrible, and I cannot bear it. Yet, when I am with you, I also bring misfortune. Look at how many terrible events have happened since you met me!"

Philomela wailed and stammered over her words. Zafira just stood frozen, her mouth gaping. Zafira wished she could think of the right thing to say, knowing that Yaya would know precisely how to help the princess.

"I must examine the signs and the obstacles," Philomela added. "I am certain now. It is the gods who want to destroy me! If not today, tomorrow, or soon after…they will succeed. I should disappear so my destiny does not affect anyone but me!"

"But—" Zafira couldn't even get two words out before Philomela went on. It was as if the princess had to spew out all her emotions, or they would choke her.

"Yes, disappear," the princess continued. "Perhaps I should destroy myself before the doomed circumstances occur? Why, I could throw myself off the cliffs above the caves of the Acropolis. Or I could return to the sea and swim until I can breathe no more. Oh, wretched life! I am a curse for all who know me!" Philomela moaned and fell into a pile, bawling.

She wants to kill herself?!?

Zafira rushed over to hug Philomela again. "Philomela, don't be silly. You're not a curse. You're a sweet person; you really are. Someone is just trying to get to you. But you can't let them. I mean…look, you saved me! Lots of times, don't you remember? And if you were so cursed, don't you think we would have already been killed by the harpy, strangled by the vine creature, or even buried under the rubble?"

Philomela continued crying. "You do not understand, Zafira."

"But I think I *do* understand. I think you've actually been my lucky charm through all these crazy things! And if you can be that for me, maybe that's what you'll be for Procne and your family…and for everyone!"

Philomela had quieted down. "Oh, dear Zafira, you are so lovely and so good. It is for this very reason I now know what I truly must do. That is, I will return to the palace and embrace what awaits me. Yes, it will be so." Philomela was nodding furiously as if she was still trying to convince herself.

Philomela got up and wiped her face. Zafira stood next to her, holding the princess by her left shoulder.

This poor girl. I feel so bad for her!

Zafira tightened her grip, and Philomela smiled.

"Thank you, Zafira," Philomela said. "But, yes, I'm sure. The palace is where I belong, where I need to be. I can only hope and beg that you will forgive me for what I have made you endure today. But now, I am certain. I know my family is distraught. I must relieve them of that pain. Also, we cannot ignore the reality that, soon, these fields will be filled with royal guards searching for me. This will only delay your quest even more. This, I cannot allow. No, I *must* go home. As you have a home you must return to, so have I."

"But what are you going to tell your family? And what are you going to do about all that stuff with your sister?"

"Fear not, my dear friend, I will create a story to explain my absence and where I have been. They will believe me. Then, I will do everything in my power to be the best daughter, sister, and princess I can be. I will face my future with dignity and strength. That is all… And indeed, I believe it will be for the best."

Zafira handed Philomela the water bottle, and the princess took a small sip of the remaining water. Then, in between short inhales, Philomela told Zafira where she could find nearby water springs and wells, as well as fig trees. She also gave Zafira her small bag with extra dried fruit, nuts, and even her prayer figurines.

"May they bless you and protect you always, friend," Philomela said with fresh tears. "It will be night soon. If I hurry, I can perhaps enter the gate before the deep darkness. And I hope you will find your way before then, too!" She gulped.

It was time to say goodbye. She grabbed Zafira and hugged her tight, leaving a trail of tears on Zafira's neck.

"Perhaps we will meet again in a much better situation. You are…you are…" But Philomela didn't finish. She grabbed Zafira by the shoulders and kissed her cheeks repeatedly before giving her another warm hug.

Zafira hugged back and whispered, "Bye, Philomela. I'll miss you." It was true. She may have wanted to ditch her before, but after all they had been through together, a real friendship had sprouted. Well, as real as possible in a dream.

Zafira decided she'd devote a special section to her in her dream journal tomorrow. She never wanted to forget this brave princess who became her friend.

Philomela was the first to turn and run away. As she faded into the distance, Zafira knew her dream was ending.

Okay, Zaffy... Now it's really time. You've seen what life is like back here, whenever this is! And you've got lots of stuff to ask Yaya about. Plus, you met a nice girl, learned lots about her, and even survived all that crazy stuff. But now it's time to just wake up!

Zafira shut her eyes tight and started to spin around.

So, wake up! Wake up, Zaffy! WAKE UP!!!

Nothing happened. Zafira was still on that hill overlooking the ancient Aegean Sea. She had no idea what to do.

So, she walked down the hill—back the way they came. She figured when it was really time to wake up, she would. Until then, she might as well keep trekking.

She picked up a tiny, light purple flower and twirled it around. She tried to distract herself by listing all the flowers she knew.

Roses. Sunflowers. Tulips. Daisies. Orchids.

But seeing as she was never good at identifying flowers, that didn't last long. She sighed.

Zafira looked around. She was surrounded by empty fields, empty hills, and empty woods. It was shocking how deserted it was.

So shocking that when she actually saw a speck of a farmer up ahead walking with his donkey, she flinched. The man looked like he was walking toward her, or rather *speed-walking*. In fact, he reached her and went past her in what seemed like a second.

That's weird.

Zafira shrugged and kept ambling along. But then, seconds later, she saw a flock of birds zoom by at lightspeed, too. And then a herd of goats also flashed by on a nearby hill. It was like everything was going in fast forward.

Well, that's dreaming for you.

Zafira hoped it meant it was almost time to wake up.

In no time, she found herself at the base of the Acropolis again. She shrugged and figured she might as well go back in.

How long is this dream going to last?

Zafira passed through the Snake Doorway. At least now, everything around her seemed to be moving at a normal pace again.

The Acropolis was full of people carrying things, pushing carts, or simply milling about. There were also lots of workers and soldiers busily rebuilding the damaged buildings. Zafira made her way straight toward the palace.

Just as she was about to go up the enormous, open entrance into the palace, she heard a distinctive chirp from up above. She glanced up and saw her blue-patched bird friend swooping around.

"Mr. Bird! You're back," Zafira cried out.

With its now trademark swoop and turn, Zafira could tell the bird wanted her to follow it. So, she did.

Mr. Bird led her deeper into the palace. They meandered their way through the spacious courtyards and elaborate walkways.

When Zafira was in the palace before, it was dark and shadowy, but she could see its rich decoration. However, it was shockingly over the top in the daylight. Painted decorations, gold, silver, and ivory were everywhere, and the whole place seemed to glimmer and sparkle.

All of a sudden, Mr. Bird's chirps turned into rhythmic trills, like in a song. Then, like a boomerang, Philomela came flying around a corner.

"Oh! It is true! I thought I heard our bird. I cannot

believe it!" Philomela almost tackled Zafira.

The princess looked so pretty. She wore a beautiful, striped yellow-blue-and-green dress. Her golden curls bounced with every step, and the only things more gleaming than her hair were the layers of gold jewelry on her neck, ears, arms, and wrists.

Philomela scanned the area as if checking to ensure no one was nearby. She squeezed Zafira tightly. Then, Philomela pulled Zafira into an isolated corridor.

"Oh, my dear, beloved friend, you returned! But why? It is not safe here! I have so much to tell you! But where did you go? Why have you not already returned to your home?"

"Well, it's only been a few hours, Philomela. I mean, it didn't even really get dark yet," Zafira replied.

"What do you mean, Zafira?" Philomela looked at her with shock and confusion. "Why, nine days have passed since we parted."

CHAPTER 16: A WEDDING AND MORE

Nine days?!? Zafira scoffed. Seriously, nine days? That's why everything seemed to be going so fast. I must have fast-forwarded myself in this dream!

Zafira barely had time to wonder why before Philomela grabbed her and pulled her down several hallways and across a few courtyards. Soon, they had zig-zagged their way to the royal bed chambers in the back corner of the palace.

When they got into Philomela's room, the princess turned to face Zafira with tear-stained cheeks. Zafira didn't even realize she had been crying.

"Oh, Zafira. It is all so terrible. The prophecy is true and has already begun!" Philomela crumbled onto a wooden stool by the built-in bed.

"What? What do you mean?" Zafira knelt down next to her. "What happened when you got back?"

"When I arrived, my parents were very worried and angry at my disappearance. They thought I had been kidnapped or killed in the earthquake," Philomela said in between tearful sobs. "At first, they were overcome with relief to see me safe. However, those emotions were soon replaced with anger."

"Why?" Zafira asked. "What did you tell them?"

"I said I had overslept and missed the festival. This much was certainly true, but I had to fabricate most of the rest because I knew they would not believe any aspects to do with you, a heroine from the future." Philomela cleared her throat and went on. "So, I said that in my sadness and remorse, I began wandering around the city and even went beyond the limits of the outer wall. It was already late when I realized how far I had gone, so I slept under a tree."

Philomela blew her nose on a small linen cloth before continuing. "I told them I had planned to re-enter the citadel in the early morning. However, when the earthquake occurred, a heavy branch from the tree fell on my head, and I got disorientated. I told them I roamed the fields outside of Athens for a long while until I finally remembered my way home. And that is when I returned to the Acropolis."

Zafira actually thought it was pretty believable and said so. Apparently, it wasn't, and Philomela's parents punished her for three days. The princess hadn't been allowed to leave her room or see anyone, especially Procne.

"Truly, this was terrible. Yet there is more...much worse!"

"What's worse? Tell me already!" Zafira stood up and paced the room. She nibbled on her cuticles again while waiting for Philomela to finish her story.

"My absence served as a warning to my father of how important it is to secure his children's matrimonies as quickly as possible to continue the lineage of our family. So, thinking they may have lost one of their only two daughters, my father decided to hurry my sister's wedding for political and security reasons."

"Oh no!" Zafira stopped and faced Philomela. "Do you mean Procne is already—?"

"Married? Yes!" Philomela shrieked.

Zafira gulped hard, putting her hand on her chest.

Philomela shook her head and continued. "You see, my father decided to set Procne's wedding just three days after my return. Even though they saw I was safe and there was no danger, they still did it. They even went against tradition by not waiting until winter!"

"I didn't know what was taking place," Philomela went on, "until my mother came to my room on the third day of my punishment, carrying a beautiful dark blue-and-red dress. It was so splendid—the patterns, the color, the finest wool. I could not understand what it was for. Then, she explained that I was to wear it because Procne was to marry Tereus later that day!"

A few tears fell from Philomela's eyes as she told Zafira how she had begged her mother to stop the wedding. She even tried to tell her all about the prophecy. But her mother had thought she was being overly emotional and jealous.

Zafira stood like a confused statue in the middle of the room, her hand on her forehead. It was difficult to take it all in and make sense of where her dream was going.

"Oh, why could she not understand?" Philomela covered her face with her hands. "Zafira, I was not even allowed to talk to Procne, for she was getting ready in a separate part of the palace, where I was forbidden to go."

Philomela paced her room. "Procne was being ritually prepared and bathed by the elderly women of the royal family. I only saw her when she was carried into the *megaron*—the main hall—where the ceremony and celebration occurred. Procne was exquisite, with her elegant gown, magnificent jewels, and her beautiful hair. But I could see that she was scared and unsure."

Philomela clasped her throat like she was swallowing something disgusting. "Oh Zafira, our eyes connected for a brief moment, and it was almost as if she was saying: 'Help me! Help me!' And I could do nothing! Oh, and that brutal, disgusting man, Tereus! He was always next to her, gripping her tightly. He was grinning, clapping to the wedding hymns, or stuffing his face with sesame seed cakes. I hated him instantly. I even wanted to kill him with my own two hands, Zafira! Truly, I did! Oh, it was one of the worst days of my life!"

Philomela wilted onto her bed, crying again.

Zafira sensed there was even more to be shared. "Where's Procne now?"

Philomela sniffled. "The custom is that Procne must move into Tereus's house. Tereus lives in Thrace—in the north. It is several days journey by ship. Their departure has been delayed because of all the necessary naval preparations. But now—" Philomela stifled a sob. "Oh, wretched sight! They are ready to leave by morning's light!"

Oh, man! Zafira knew she'd have to come up with something…and fast.

"But Zafira, there is something else," Philomela added. "Procne visited me secretly in my bed chamber two nights ago when Tereus and my father were drinking wine."

"What did she tell you?"

"It is even worse than what I had imagined. Tereus is an animal! He talks badly to her, he screams at her, and when he gets furious, he becomes physically violent. He is a complete monster! My poor sister is desperate and sad. I wish I could help her, but I know not what to do!"

He hits her? That pig! We have to help Procne.

Zafira bent down and hugged her friend. "Philomela, we're going to help her, I promise. I came here to help you, and I guess I now know that means also helping Procne. I don't know how we'll do that, but I'm sure we'll think of something."

Zafira tried one plan after another: going to Philomela's parents and making them believe everything, kidnapping Procne, or even trying to scare Tereus away.

But Philomela was beyond hopeless.

"It is all futile, Zafira. The prophecy has begun, and now, Procne and I must merely wait to become these wretched creatures that will do terrible things to our family and to Athens." She rolled over, face down on her bed, sobbing.

Zafira wouldn't give up. "Come on, Philomela. It's not hopeless. Trust me!" Zafira paced figure-eights in the room.

"Okay, since Procne and Tereus are leaving tomorrow morning, we have to do something tonight."

Philomela sniffled and inhaled short, shallow breaths.

Zafira strategized aloud. "So, tonight, tonight... Let's see." She snapped her fingers and faced Philomela, who sat up again. "Does Tereus share a room with your sister?"

"No. Royal couples have a common room, each with their own chambers to sleep in. Further, while they are still in my father's palace, it was agreed that Procne would remain in her own bed chamber. It will be different when they arrive at Tereus's palace. Why?"

"Well, I'm invisible, right? Don't you remember how scared Procne got when she only saw your floating nightgown without me?"

Philomela shrugged half-heartedly, but Zafira was on a roll.

"Imagine if I go to Tereus's room tonight, all ghost-like,

and threaten him in the creepiest way possible. Maybe I could throw things at him and say things like: 'Leave Procne or face death!' Or 'Athena is angry, and you have to leave Athens alone and never come back!'" She used her deepest, most gurgly voice. "I mean, we can make up our own prophecy to scare him the same way it scared you," Zafira shrugged and grinned, full of hope.

But Philomela looked unconvinced. "Absolutely not, Zafira. You do not know how monstrous this man is. He is dangerous and vicious. Even if he cannot see you, he can try to hurt you, especially if threatened. I will not allow that!"

"But if we make him think he's going crazy, he won't know what to do. And then no one will believe him. Plus, as soon as I scare him enough, I'll take off your clothes, which will be on top of mine. So, he won't even be able to see me to hurt me. Come on, I think it's the best chance we've got!"

Philomela raised one eyebrow slightly; that was all Zafira needed to see. There was a glimmer of hope.

So, Zafira spent the next few minutes solidifying the plan and reassuring Philomela. It took a little while more, but the princess was ultimately convinced.

They decided that Zafira would sneak into Tereus's room late that night and do her best to scare him. If Zafira felt in danger at any point, she'd leave before anything bad happened. She promised the princess.

"Everything will be fine, Philomela," Zafira said. She knew it was true. For the first time in this crazy, unexpected dream, she felt positive and certain. "So, I guess all we need to do is just wait until Tereus goes to bed, and then—"

But when Zafira turned around, Philomela was gone.

"Philomela?" Zafira called out, but Philomela's bedroom was fading away as if it was being sucked into the background.

Zafira knew what was happening.

No, no, no…

It was too late. The last thing she heard was a cackle of birds in the distance before she was swept up in a whirlwind of darkness.

And then she woke up in her own bed.

PART TWO:

ZAFIRA AND THE GIRLS

CHAPTER 17: ANXIOUS AND AWAKE

Zafira flung the covers off and jumped out of bed. Slivers of sunlight peeked through her blinds, making the dust in her room sparkle like diamonds. But this time, she wouldn't try to catch it and count all her 'treasure'—like she used to do with Yaya. There was no time for silly games. No, she had to get back to ancient Greece to find out what happened to the girls—and fast.

She knew exactly what she needed to do.

As usual, her mom was already at work, but she went right into her parents' bedroom, where her dad was shaving.

"Morning, hon," Stelios said and tapped his razor on the side of the sink.

Zafira coughed once, then three more times in succession. "Dad, my throat is killing me, and my head kinda hurts, too."

"Oh, sweetie, do you think you're sick?"

Her dad was usually a much easier sell than her nurse mom for things like this. It helped this time that Zafira really did look believably agitated and even felt a little nauseous.

Stelios led her back to bed and told her he would call her in sick at school and also call Yaya to stay with her. He then kissed her goodbye, and Zafira rolled over on her side.

But, try as she might, she just couldn't fall asleep. By the time Yaya came over, Zafira had been tossing and turning for over an hour. She had built up quite a sweat, which was convenient since she was pretending to be sick.

As her grandma tip-toed quietly into her room, Zafira sat up. "It's okay, Yaya. I'm awake."

"I'm sorry you're not feeling well, sweetie," Yaya said. She placed a glass of water on Zafira's nightstand and then sat on the end of Zafira's bed. "I'm going to make you some soup right away. Is there anything else you need?"

Zafira sat up more and hugged her knees. "Actually, would you mind sitting with me for a bit?"

"Sure, *gliki mou.*" Yaya moved up next to Zafira's pillow, leaning back on Zafira's headboard and putting her arm around Zafira. "Are you sure nothing else is wrong, my love?"

"Mmm-hmm. I was wondering if you could maybe tell me one of your stories... You know, to help me fall asleep?"

"Well, let me get you something to eat first—"

But Zafira was too impatient. "Yaya, what came before Classical Greece?" She blurted out.

The question surprised Yaya. "Oh, Zafira," she said and chuckled. "You're always thinking about the past! But not now, sweetie. Let's not fill your head with history today, okay?" Yaya got up and re-tucked Zafira in.

Zafira persisted. "Please, Yaya. Just a few minutes? And then I promise I'll rest. *Pleee-ase?*"

Yaya heaved a deep sigh and sat down in the overstuffed armchair by Zafira's bed.

"Okay, Zaffy," She cleared her throat and started. "So,

before Classical Greece, huh? Well, darling, Athens goes back a *looooong* way. We talked about the Parthenon yesterday. So, that was built in the mid-400s B.C.E. Do you remember what that means?"

Zafira nodded with enthusiasm.

"Well, actually, honey," Yaya added, "it was *re*built then, because there was evidence that an earlier, older temple existed on the Acropolis but was destroyed in a big war with a civilization called the Persians. That war happened many years prior. Actually, do you remember that cool movie called *300*?"

"Totally! I loved that movie! And I loved that Dad let me watch something so violent," Zafira replied with a smirk.

"True, but you know...the Classics professor in him overshadows everything else," Yaya sighed and chuckled. "So, that movie was based on an important battle—the Battle of Thermopylae—which happened during the Persian War. In fact, your Theo Leo's name, Leonidas, comes from one of the great heroes of that war."

"Cool."

Yaya smiled, but there was worry in her eyes. She half-nodded before going on. "Anyway, the earlier temple on the Acropolis, among other things, was destroyed during that war. But it was later reconstructed as the resilient, beautiful temple we know today. It was rebuilt by the city's ruler, a man called Pericles, in around 450 B.C.E. All of this was the Classical Period, as I've told you before."

Zafira leaned on her side, urging her grandma to keep going.

"But two of the earliest Greek civilizations lived hundreds of years *before* the Parthenon was even built. They were known as the Minoans and the Mycenaeans. They lived during a period known as The Bronze Age because they made lots of things out of bronze and other metals. The Minoans were mostly found throughout the southern islands in Greece, and the Mycenaeans were found on the mainland, like in Athens and a few other ancient cities."

Zafira bit her lip. "When did the Mice-and-nee-nums live?"

"Mice-in-eee-yaans," Yaya said, correcting her. "Good question, honey. Well, art historians have debated the exact dates since it's quite difficult to be sure because there are so few remains from that time. But usually, they say they lived from around 1600 B.C.E. to about 1200 B.C.E. It might even be earlier. So, you see, that's a thousand years *before* the Parthenon and over three thousand years before us—thirty centuries ago!"

"Wait, so let me get it straight. Back during these Mice-and...I mean, Mice-in-eee-yaans, the Acropolis still existed, but not the Parthenon, right?"

"Exactly," Yaya said. "The Parthenon wasn't built yet, but there is evidence of a temple that existed prior to the Parthenon. Before that, during Mycenaean times, the Acropolis was most likely a citadel—or walled city—which probably protected the king's castle. It's not certain, but there might have been a temple back then as well, although we don't know if it was for Athena. See, we aren't sure if the Mycenaeans believed in the same mythological gods that Classical Greeks did. But it's a possibility."

"A citadel? The king?" Zafira talked out loud while she kept piecing things together.

"Yes," Yaya went on. "You see, hundreds of years before Athens became a democracy, where people could vote for their leaders, the city was said to have been ruled by many kings, like even Theseus, remember? From the labyrinth with the minotaur?"

"Yup!" Zafira beamed but then forced out a fake cough to keep up the sick pretense.

Yaya handed her the glass of water. "Well," she continued, "these kings wanted big palaces and tall, huge walls to surround and protect their palaces and cities. The Mycenaeans were said to have been great warriors and engineers. How they used stones to build their walls, gates, and even tombs is still remarkable today."

Stone walls and stone gates? How did I dream it if I didn't actually know it?!?

Zafira's mind raced through the possibilities. *Did I learn it from Dad once and just forgot? Or read it in one of Yaya's books?*

In her eagerness, Zafira almost rolled off the edge of her bed.

"Zaffy, if you could have seen how big and massive some of these stones were, you'd think only a *giant* could lift and build with those!" Yaya said, shaking her head in amazement. "But they did it, and, in fact, their stonework is called 'cyclopean masonry' because it would take a mythical giant creature like Cyclops to lift and build structures with those stones. They really were *that big*, Zaffy."

Oh, I know EXACTLY how big and massive those stones and those walls were!

Zafira almost wanted to tell Yaya everything about her dream, but she also didn't want her to stop explaining.

"Sweetie, you don't seem to be getting any more tired. How about this," Yaya said, standing up. "I'm going to go get you some tea, and I'll bring up one of your dad's textbooks to show you some stuff from the Mycenaeans. Then, you promise me you'll try to sleep?"

Zafira promised. *If only Yaya knew how much I really, really want to get back to sleep!*

Yaya was back in no time. She continued her history lesson as Zafira sat in bed, drinking her tea and munching on cinnamon-and-butter toast.

"Also, Zaffy, there aren't many documents left over from Mycenaean times because Greece went into their Dark Ages for hundreds of years afterward. Dark Ages means that there was little cultural development, and hardly anything was documented," Yaya added. "But archeologists, just in the past couple hundred years, have dug up some amazing finds from before those Dark Ages. Here, let me show you."

She placed an art history book on the edge of Zafira's bed and pointed to a giant archway. It looked like the gate Zafira called the Snake Doorway, except instead of two snakes, this one had two lions—whose heads were missing—facing a column. But the stones were stacked similarly over the top of the massive doorway.

"This is called *The Lion Gate,* and it was the entrance to the citadel in the city of Mycenae," Yaya explained. "It's one of the best remaining structures which show Mycenaean cyclopean masonry. I mean…look at the size of those stones!"

Zafira peered over, trailing crumbs over the ancient arch.

"And, do you see how this archway has a big stone slab on top, supported by two vertical slabs on the side?" Yaya asked, and Zafira nodded in slow motion. "Well, honey, that might not seem so impressive nowadays, what with all our skyscrapers and such. But back then—remember over three thousand years ago—this was very innovative."

Yaya explained they called that architectural technique

'post-and-lintel,' which included a top, horizontal stone called a 'lintel,' and two vertical columns called 'posts'—kind of like goal posts in soccer.

"Now, this alone wasn't so complex, but the positioning of the stones above the post-and-lintel made it really cool. See how they slowly get closer until they form a triangle shape?" Yaya asked again, and Zafira murmured a yes.

"Well, that allowed them to redistribute the weight of the heavy stones in the gateway. This top part is known as a 'corbelled arch,' and the triangle part in the middle—the one here with the two lions," she tapped the photo, "that's known as a 'relieving triangle.' I know all of these terms are a bit confusing, Zaffy, but basically, you put it all together, and it created a really, really strong gateway. I mean…wow! It's still upright today!"

Zafira stared at an almost exact replica of the gate she had gone through at the Acropolis in her dream.

Did I go through a gate like this in ancient Athens instead of ancient Mycenae?

Zafira was left wondering while Yaya went on. "So, you see, Zaffy, the Mycenaeans were famous for their architecture, both in their strongly fortified citadels and their innovative building techniques. But they were also famous for their pottery and metalwork. Look at these pictures…"

Yaya leaned over to show her several photographs, including a delicate golden cup, a pair of gold earrings, a bronze and gold dagger, and a golden face mask.

"Remember before, Zaffy, when I said the Mycenaeans lived in a time known as the Bronze Age?"

"Yup," Zafira replied, not missing a beat.

"Well, this is why," Yaya pointed to the images again. "Just look at what they could already do with gold, silver, and bronze. They loved shaping and designing their metals.

And they especially loved their gold!"

Boy, did they ever!

Zafira turned to put her empty mug and plate on her bedside table. She then snuggled under her covers, hanging on to her grandma's every word, even though the tea was beginning to lull her a bit.

Yaya lowered her voice and slowly continued. "They also loved painting their vases and even had special ceremonial cups shaped like animals. They called those 'rhytons.' Take a peek at this one in the shape of a bull's head." She held the book up, and Zafira gasped.

Rhytons! But how could I have dreamt all this if I had never learned it before?

Zafira knew she'd have to tell Yaya about her dream as soon as she returned and finished helping Philomela.

"And you know, Zaffy, many of their gold pieces were found in these special tombs that the Mycenaeans built. They were called 'beehive tombs' because of their funny shapes. They were these circular, domed tombs that were mostly underground—"

Zafira zoned out briefly, her mind racing, trying to piece together everything she had seen and done in her dream.

Yaya continued, oblivious to Zafira's distraction. "—where they probably buried their kings. And so, like I said before, during Mycenaean times, Athens was most likely ruled by a king."

"A great example of a Mycenaean king can be found in the stories connected to the Trojan War," Yaya added. "A beautiful girl called Helen of Troy fell in love with a Trojan boy named Paris, even though she was married to a Greek king called Menelaus. Menelaus's brother was King Agamemnon, one of the most famous Mycenaean kings. In fact, he was the king of the actual city called Mycenae, one of the most important cities at that time, and where the name came from. This golden death mask is said to be of him, although that's still debated."

Yaya pointed to a photo, and Zafira stared at a thin, golden mask. It had closed eyes, a crooked nose, a long mustache, a tight-lipped mouth, and two strangely disconnected ears.

The King of Mycenae?

"But Mycenae wasn't the only important city at that time. There was Tiryns, Thebes, and even, of course, Athens, where the old Mycenaean king of Athens lived..."

Zafira was getting sleepier and sleepier.

The old Mycenaean king of Athens? Could King Pandion, Philomela's dad, have been one of those? But how could I know all this? How could I have invented all this? How—

But with those last thoughts, Zafira finally drifted off to sleep.

CHAPTER 18: PROCNE AND ITYS

Zafira found herself in the middle of a dark, dense forest.

She first saw the denim bag on the ground next to her. All her things were there, including the still almost-empty water bottle, the flashlight, and Philomela's figurines.

Zafira took a cleansing breath, determined and ready to find the girls again. She understood that, for the first time in one of her dreams, it wasn't just about what she would see or do for *herself*. It was about what she could do for *them*. And she liked the way that sounded.

Zafira wandered around. "Hello? Can anyone hear me? Philomela? Mr. Bird? Anyone?" She didn't hear anything.

Zafira needed to figure out which way to go. She could end up deeper in the forest if she went wrong. She circled around, but it all seemed the same, without a path or clearing in sight.

Then, she heard several female voices in the distance and raced toward them. Zafira soon came across a narrow path that cut through the trees. Ahead of her, she spotted three young women walking together. She rushed to get closer but stayed out of sight in case her invisibility didn't work anymore.

Zafira followed along carefully and caught random words from the women's conversation, including 'clean,' 'hidden,' 'palace,' and 'tired.' She also saw that two of the women carried baskets full of dirty rags, and all three wore long, stained, and ripped dresses. One of the women held a large, brown, wrapped bundle tied up with a rope.

Zafira sighed with relief when she heard the word 'palace.' But there was an itchy, funny feeling she couldn't shake.

Like, why is there a forest on the Acropolis? That definitely wasn't here before.

Plus, Zafira couldn't be sure, but it seemed like there was a different accent in the way these women talked compared to the way Philomela did. But Zafira shrugged it off and followed them.

After a short while, the group came out of the forest. Zafira blinked a few times at the bright light. When her eyes adjusted, she rubbed them in disbelief.

High on the edge of a cliff overlooking the sea was a slightly smaller palace than the one on the Acropolis. Zafira stumbled forward as the three women went straight toward the high-walled structure.

When they reached the enormous gate, which had no elaborately carved stones on top, the guards approached them. Zafira hid behind a nearby tree while the three women were questioned. She overheard them saying they had been cleaning the tower castle in the forest and were returning to the palace for the night. The guards asked them a few more questions before letting them in.

This definitely wasn't the Acropolis.

But if it isn't Philomela's palace, then whose is it?

Zafira looked up at the tall wall. Then she realized it was time to test her invisibility again. She took a deep breath and stepped out from behind the tree.

The guards didn't move. In fact, their expressions of misery and boredom didn't flinch an inch.

Zafira exhaled and shuffled through the gate. Once inside, she stumbled through a spacious courtyard, a bright colonnade, and finally into a decorative, semi-enclosed room. Like the one on the Acropolis, this palace was also colorful and full of decoration. But it didn't have as much gold or ivory as Philomela's palace.

Zafira wandered around, letting her eyes jump from the blue, red, and yellow grid-like designs on the floor to the many battle scenes painted on the walls. The ceiling and column tops were painted with large circles, waves, squares, curlicues, and stars.

But from every room or courtyard, Zafira always saw the fortified wall in the distance. It made the whole building feel like a prison.

Philomela's palace was much warmer and cozier.

A woman's voice from across the courtyard caught Zafira's attention. She rushed over and saw a young woman wearing a long, plain, dark blue dress. The gown had a narrow waist and was shaped like a bell. It was like all the other dresses Zafira had seen so far—another clue that, at least, she was still in ancient Greece.

The woman was also wearing a simple golden necklace. But above her neck, Zafira instantly recognized the long, curly auburn hair, olive skin, brown eyes, and those distinctive small ears.

Procne!

Zafira stared as Philomela's older sister talked to a nearby servant. Even though Zafira had seen her nine days earlier—if no other time had passed in this dream—Procne seemed thinner, scruffier, and very sad.

When the servant left, Zafira trailed Procne through the palace. They passed several rooms and continued down a long corridor. Procne stopped outside the door of a dark room. She hurried in, and Zafira followed. It only took a second for Zafira to see what was inside: a sleeping child.

Procne covered the boy, who looked about two or three years old. She then kissed her fingers and placed them lovingly on his forehead. She stayed a few more seconds, staring with what had to be a mother's love and concern, before leaving the room.

That can't be her son...unless...oh no! Did I come back years later?

Zafira felt woozy and dazed. She followed Procne to her bedroom.

Once they were inside, Procne began to organize things. Her room was a lot like Philomela's. It was brightly decorated, and the walls were painted with oversized framed panels of trees, hills, and a sea full of tiny painted fish. A bed, a bench, and a table were built into the walls, and there was even a very similar bath corner.

The most significant difference was that there weren't any windows up near the ceiling. Instead, light was coming in from an opening in the ceiling over the bathtub, like a giant ancient skylight.

As Procne moved around the room, Zafira wondered how to get Procne to see her.

Procne suddenly burst into tears. She dropped the pillow she was holding and fell into a heap on the floor, sobbing uncontrollably.

Zafira rushed over.

"Procne! Procne! It's me, Zafira? Your sister's friend?

Can you hear me?" Zafira tried to lean down to hug the wailing princess, but Procne didn't stop crying. She couldn't hear or feel anything.

Except for her own pain.

Zafira racked her brain, thinking of something to get the princess's attention. She leaned down, picked up a sandal, and tossed it into the corner with a bang.

Procne looked up, forlorn and hopeless. She glanced at the sandal but didn't even seem to care why it was now in a different place.

Zafira paced the room, hoping for some inspiration. What was it that had made Philomela see her?

Well, besides being in a near-death experience with a crazy bird-woman, I can't think of anything else.

A near-death experience! That might be it!

Zafira realized she hadn't had that with anyone else out here, and maybe that was what it would take for people to see her. Maybe in moments of extreme stress, her invisibility wore off?

She had to find out. She needed to put Procne in some kind of danger, and then, *maybe* then, she would see her? It couldn't hurt to try...or at least Zafira hoped she wouldn't hurt *her* trying.

Zafira rummaged through her bag and found the matches. She hesitated for a second, but as the young princess continued to sob in a ball on the floor, Zafira knew she had to talk to her to help her. So, without stopping to think, Zafira knelt down and lit a wool blanket on the floor next to Procne.

It erupted in flames, and Procne almost rolled into the fire in her surprise. Thankfully, she didn't and scooted back away from the blaze. She didn't scream or run. Instead, she stared at the glow, transfixed and shocked.

Zafira stomped on the small fire, but a tiny spark bounced onto the hem of her jeans and began to burn. She screamed, fell to the ground, rolled over, and beat the spark with her hands. The tiny blaze disappeared as quickly as it had started, and Zafira heaved a sigh of relief.

She checked out the tiny burn mark on the bottom of her jeans.

I really need to stop playing with fire out here.

Zafira chuckled to herself before turning toward Procne, hoping at least her risky and dangerous plan had worked.

It had. Procne had stopped crying and was staring at Zafira with a gaping mouth.

CHAPTER 19: DEATH AND SADNESS

Zafira rolled over and sat kneeling with her hands on her lap. She was so anxious to talk, so she took a deep breath, hoping Procne would believe her as easily as her sister had.

"Procne, please don't be afraid," Zafira said, trying to control and slow her speech. "My name is Zafira. I don't know if you remember me, but I'm Philomela's friend. She told you about me...about a week ago? And told you that I was from the future? Does that sound familiar?" She paused to see if anything was going in.

Procne stared in silence.

Zafira went on. She reminded Procne about the harpy attack and what Philomela had told her sister. "So, since you can see me now, you'll believe that I'm not a ghost. I'm real. And Philomela was telling the truth." Zafira exhaled and gazed toward Procne, anxious to see the princess's reaction.

Procne continued to stare, paralyzed. Then her face scrunched up into another wail. This time though, she screamed her sister's name in between sobs.

"Philomela! Oh, Philomela!"

Zafira felt a sharp pang. Something wasn't right. For the first time, she feared the worst. "Wait, did something happen to Philomela?"

Procne just balled herself up again. Zafira rushed over, fell beside her, and shook her gently but firmly.

"Procne, listen to me. You have to listen to me. What happened to Philomela?" It took several minutes, more strength, and even a couple of pinches before Procne responded.

"My dear sister...my beloved Philomela. She is gone; she is gone!"

"What do you mean, 'gone'?" Zafira asked, her face creased in confusion. "Where did she go?"

"Hades!" Procne yelled and exploded into tears again.

"Wait...Hades? Isn't that the place where your dead people go?" Zafira asked.

Procne nodded.

Oh, shoot! I did wake up way later. But wait...Philomela died?

Zafira knew this was all imaginary, but she still couldn't shake her sadness.

"But I was just with her a couple hours ago!" Zafira blurted out.

Procne stared at Zafira in disbelief, her face stained with tears. "You say you were with Philomela recently? How can you say such terrible things? Why have you come to torment me? To torture me? Have I not suffered enough?"

"Torture you? Listen, Procne, I don't know what happened, but I'm here to *help* you."

Zafira tried to explain all that had happened in her first dream, including more about the harpy, the vine creature, the temple, the earthquake, escaping Athens, and Philomela's return to the palace. Zafira also told Procne how

Philomela had told Zafira about the wedding, Tereus, and their plan to save her.

Procne continued to stare, horrified. After what seemed like forever, she finally opened her mouth and stuttered a response in a low whisper. "Five summers have passed since my wedding. Five. Long. Summers."

Five years? Five years have passed?!?

Zafira had truly hoped to save both girls and see Philomela again. She swallowed her shock and disappointment.

Procne coughed and continued. "I left Athens and my father's palace on a ship with my husband Tereus a few days after the wedding ceremony. Nothing changed that—as you would have me believe. Philomela wept and was sad, but she saw me leave. After, I did not see my dear sister for five summer suns. I birthed my son, Itys, and still never saw my sister. Only recently, I finally convinced my husband to travel back and ask my father to allow Philomela to visit me here."

"Here?" Zafira asked.

"Yes, here," Procne replied. "In Thrace, the kingdom ruled by my husband, Tereus. You are in the great citadel palace of Thrace, on the sea, north of Athens."

It all made sense: the forest, the different palace, and even the accents. Zafira had woken up in another part of Mycenaean Greece five years later.

"Tereus returned from Athens only weeks ago with the poisonous news. There was a funeral. Philomela died...from grief! Oh, wretched pain! My matrimony, which fulfilled some crazy prophecy...this...this was the reason Philomela died. Don't you see? I killed my sister!" Procne screeched out the last words and started sobbing again.

Zafira was speechless.

But Procne wasn't. It was like she had rediscovered her ability to speak. She described everything she had been through and everything she had suffered. It poured out of her like an oozing wound. She said she wished she had died instead of Philomela.

"Perhaps I was jealous of her superior beauty, or perhaps I was always a terrible sister. Yet, only after my dreadful wedding and my voyage to this prison of a palace did I begin to see my past mistakes and how cruel I had been to her. How I did regret it and how I did miss her! All I wanted was to be reunited with my sister...to see her beautiful face and hear her lovely voice."

Procne sniffled and went on. "And now...what pain, what suffering! She is gone! Further, I must raise a son under the darkness of misery and anguish! And I will forever be burdened not only with a savage for a husband but with a sisterless existence!"

After she had spewed out what seemed like all she could, Procne collapsed onto her bed. She covered her face with her hands and cried with gut-wrenching desperation.

If Philomela died, then what am I doing back here?

Zafira was in a trance when a loud, phlegmy, sticky voice echoed outside Procne's room.

"Procne! Where are you, woman?"

Procne gasped and rubbed the tears from her eyes. "He is coming! He is near!"

Zafira almost choked. *Tereus!*

Before Zafira could hide, Tereus strutted through the doorway. She held her breath, even though he probably wouldn't be able to see her and definitely wouldn't be able to hear her.

"Wife, why are you not being prepared for dinner?" Tereus circled around the room.

Zafira exhaled. Tereus wasn't a giant monster. He was a short, bald, chunky, sweaty man whose horrible smell followed him like a stinky shadow.

He wore a knee-high, colorful, belted tunic that reminded Zafira of a hilarious, old-fashioned, mid-thigh bathrobe she had once seen at a Halloween party. But when Zafira saw what was on his head, she almost burst out laughing. He wore a tall, pointy, golden crown with a picture of a charging bull hammered in on it.

How could Procne—or anyone really—be scared of this little pee-wee?

Tereus kept droning on. "Come now, where is your servant? Must I once again eat with that face of yours in front of me? Your tears disgust me." He ran a finger over one of the tables like he was inspecting it for dust.

"I have endured your mourning long enough. You must wash up and arrange yourself, you silly woman. I want to fill my belly and quickly. Move, wife!" He grunted and left the room.

Procne jumped up, rushing around. Her tears kept falling while she ran a golden comb through her hair.

Zafira tried to console her. "Procne, are you okay? Can I do anything to help you?"

"I am late for dinner," Procne said as she scurried. "How will I ever survive another meal with this man? I still have not accepted my fate, or perhaps never will! Now, please, I beg you…you must leave the palace at once. I do not know who you are and cannot endure any more pain."

Zafira was about to reply when there was a whisper at the door. "My queen?"

"Yes? Oh, Tryphosa, is it you? Please come in at once. I need your assistance."

A very young woman entered the room. She wore a

loose, beige dress that cinched with a belt, and she had a single, long, tight braid. Surprisingly, she was carrying the same bundle Zafira had seen the servant from the forest holding: a large, brown parcel tied up with a rope.

"My queen? This is for you. It was brought by a servant who cleans and minds the tower castle. She insisted I bring it directly to you, showing it to no one." The servant handed Procne the package and bowed slightly.

As soon as Procne took it, the young girl rushed around the room and helped Procne get ready for dinner. Zafira sat back, staring at them, feeling completely lost and confused. She still didn't understand why or how her subconscious was doing all this.

That didn't matter right now. She needed to help Procne, and she wouldn't stop until she did.

CHAPTER 20: MESSAGES AND ACTIONS

When the young girl finished helping Procne, she hurried out of the room, and Zafira finally spoke up again, voicing the only doubt that kept popping up in her head.

"Procne, do you think there's any way that maybe Philomela is still alive?"

Procne gawked at Zafira. Her eyes were wide and perplexed. "Strange girl, why are you here?"

Zafira didn't know what to say. "Umm...I think I'm supposed to help you both."

"Silly girl, you cannot help my sister. She is dead. Do you understand? DEAD!"

"Are you sure? Did you see her body?" Zafira pushed the issue.

"Certainly not," Procne replied with a disgusted tone. "She died in Athens. The funeral was there. It occurred before my husband's voyage. He described everything to me in great detail when he returned."

"Wait," Zafira jumped up. "You mean, you didn't actually talk to your parents about it? They weren't the ones to tell you? Have you even talked to *anyone* from Athens?"

Procne looked away, her brow slightly furrowed.

Zafira went on. "So, no one has got in touch or visited to see how you are?"

Procne was silent.

"Procne, you're putting all your trust and belief in a man like…that?" Zafira pointed toward the bedroom door, hoping she hadn't gone too far.

Procne shook her head and darted around the room, grabbing and tossing random things. "She is gone! Can you understand that?" Procne was practically shrieking now. "If she were still alive, she would be here. No, it is not possible. Please, you must not speak this way. I beg of you!"

Procne picked up the wrapped parcel and kept going. "I am sure you have good intent, yet, I must ask you…no, I must INSIST that you leave me now. I am trying to contain my tears and must go to dinner immediately!"

Procne tore at the wrapped package and took out some folded material while talking and pacing.

"She is gone! At least she is at peace. If she were alive, I would feel her. Indeed, I will admit there have been some dreams, some visions, but no…it is foolish of me, careless of me… No, I cannot, I must not…hope…"

Procne's eyes slowly narrowed in confusion as she focused on the folded cloth in her hands. She gasped loudly.

"What is that?" Zafira slid next to her and peered down at the material.

Procne shook out the folded cloth. It unveiled a tightly woven design. The wool was primarily white, but it had three shades of purple throughout to create a scene. It was like a woven cartoon strip with three parts.

She then unrolled it entirely on the bed, and the girls began to 'read' it from one side to the other.

Procne was the first one to understand the woven story. She gasped again and lurched to the side. Zafira barely caught her in time to stop her from falling over.

"What is it? What do you see?" Zafira asked while propping her up.

Procne lips moved, but no words came out.

Zafira asked again, louder. Procne just kept on staring at both the cloth and Zafira.

Zafira finally grabbed Procne by the shoulders and shook her hard. "What. Is. It?"

Procne's voice was barely a whisper. "But...it cannot be...how...yet—"

Zafira shook her again. "Procne! What is it?"

The young queen looked up at Zafira as if seeing her for the first time. "This has been woven by my sister's hand. I am certain. The weave, her distinctive style... Further, you see, she always added a little π in the bottom left of everything she wove. It used to anger me so because I could not do the same since we share the letter 'P' in our names."

Zafira studied the design and noticed a tall, narrow castle with a tower on one side. "That doesn't look like the palace on the Acropolis. Where is that?"

"That is one of King Tereus's secret hideaways. He has several all over Thrace. This particular one is unique because of the tower. It is near here—deep within the forest beyond the palace. But...could it be? Is there a way..." Procne's voice faded. Her eyes were as big as bottle caps.

Zafira looked closer at the three different scenes. The first showed a man and woman on a ship. The second showed a man attacking a woman with a small sword. The final scene was the castle. But now she also saw a woman's face in a small window in the tower of the castle. Zafira squealed.

"Philomela is in the tower!" Zafira cried out. "Don't you see, Procne? She *is* alive! She *did* come up here on a ship with Tereus. But it looks like he tried to stab her. Is that for real?!? And I think he's probably locked her away in his secret castle! But, don't you see, Procne...Philomela is *alive!*"

Procne was numb while Zafira jumped up and down. "Oh, Procne! I knew it! I knew Philomela was alive. She couldn't have died. No way! And that's why I came back here! Now it all makes sense. I'm still supposed to save her...and you!"

Procne's shock was fading. "Do you think it could be true?"

"Of course, it's true! And look, she's woven this to show us what happened and where she is! And to show us what a horrible person Tereus is. I know you already know that, but...UGGHHHH! He lied to you about your own sister's death! When all along, he had her locked up in some tower!"

Suddenly, Procne shrieked. "What a foul animal! I HATE HIM! I HATE HIM!!" Then she started to growl and pant as if releasing the beast within.

Oh no! I think she's gonna blow...

Procne was seething. "I cannot believe he would do this! He has already put me through so much pain and suffering, but this? THIS?"

Zafira leaned over to the young queen, holding and shushing her while Procne wailed, moaned, shook, and shuddered. Zafira urged her to forget about that jerk and focus on the reality that Philomela was alive.

Procne leaned on Zafira and cried some more, but Zafira could feel her getting lighter and looser. It was like the weight of her grief and guilt was evaporating right off her body.

"That's good, Procne; let it out. You've been so sad for so

long. But you see, you didn't do anything wrong. None of this is your fault." Zafira felt her nodding.

"So, come on, let's get out of here. Let's go get Philomela!" Zafira couldn't wait for a second more.

Procne pulled away and gaped at Zafira. "Itys! We must protect him as well. We must take him with us. I am not leaving this palace without him! Never!"

"Of course not," Zafira said. "We'll go get him right now."

But Procne seemed scared and unsure. "It is impossible," Procne said with a sigh. "If I do not go to this meal at once, you cannot imagine how enraged and violent Tereus will become! Further, Itys's room is beyond the dining chamber. He will see me. We are trapped and doomed!" Procne collapsed in a desperate heap.

Zafira didn't miss a beat and had already devised a plan. "Don't worry, Procne. I have the best weapon. It's what I was going to use on Tereus before all this happened."

"What?"

"My invisibility!" Zafira said. "He can't see me!"

"Why, what will you do?"

Zafira explained that they would ask Tryphosa to bring some potent sleeping herbs, which Zafira could easily pour into Tereus's drink—unnoticed—at dinner. Then, after getting Itys, they would leave the palace and get to Philomela before Tereus woke up.

"So, let's get going," Zafira added, "but first, do you need anything from your room?"

"The only thing I need from this palace is my son Itys," Procne affirmed. "Everything else can stay. Indeed, everything else can go to...go to...Hades!" The young queen inhaled deeply, grabbed her shawl, and spun out of the room.

CHAPTER 21: SNEAKING AND ESCAPING

The dining room was just as colorful and flashy as the rest of the palace. One wall was a giant open entryway. The other three walls were painted in sections: a lower level full of nature scenes; a middle section with painted scenes of people eating, drinking, and dancing; and the highest part full of geometric patterns and designs. As if that wasn't enough to make someone dizzy, the floor was also tiled in alternating blue and red squares.

A long, low table was in the center of the room. With his tall golden crown, Tereus, the Short, Fat, and Slimy sat on a low stool on one end. Procne sat on the other. Except for the dining table and several small built-in tables along two of the walls, the room was empty. It would be easy for Zafira to move around.

Procne seemed bored and tired, but Zafira knew this was all an act; underneath, she was probably anxious, excited, and full of rage. She glanced up when Zafira entered the room but concealed herself nicely by rubbing her neck and taking a sip of wine.

Zafira nodded and gave the thumbs up, patting her sweatshirt's front pocket where she had hidden the herbs Tryphosa had given to Procne.

"Servant, the king requires more wine," Procne proclaimed.

One of the waiting servants picked up a golden pitcher and topped off the king's drink.

"Oh, my!" Tereus said with a burp, prompting Zafira to scowl in disgust. "Surprises abound," he continued. "The queen notices when the king is in need. Perhaps there is hope for you, yet."

He took a sip, and Zafira was on the move as soon as the wine cup was back on the table. She crept up next to the king and breathed in slowly, trying not to gag when she got a whiff of his horrible body odor.

"What is that over there?" Procne called out.

Zafira jumped but soon realized it was only Procne pointing in the opposite direction.

A diversion! Good girl!

"What are we to see?" Tereus craned his neck and opened his already drunkenly droopy eyes.

Zafira slipped into action. She dumped the entire sack of herbs into his oversized golden cup, gave it a quick stir with her finger, and moved away—fast.

When the deed was done, Procne replied, "Oh! Perhaps my eyes have fooled me! I believed I saw a serpent in the corner." The queen shrugged and returned to her meat, sneaking a peak at Zafira from the corner of her eye.

The king burped again, took another sip, and wiped the dribbles from his chin with his short sleeve. Within minutes, his glass was empty and was already being refilled by the servant. The herb/wine mixture took effect in no time. When the king passed out, he fell sideways off his stool, taking a plate of fruit down with him. Zafira shimmied with giddy excitement in the corner.

Procne took charge. "Servants?"

Both men appeared inside.

"Please take the king to his bed chamber. He has had too much wine," Procne declared, standing up. "Thank you."

The girls left the dining room while the guards worked on hoisting up the king. He was completely knocked out.

They jogged through a few corridors and were in Itys's room in seconds. With the ease of a seasoned mother, Procne bent down to cradle her sleeping son. The toddler didn't even stir. He just naturally curved himself into his mother's embrace.

"Oh, wait," Zafira whispered. "I didn't think about this part. How are we supposed to get through the palace and out the main gate? There are servants and guards everywhere!"

"Do not worry. I am the queen. No one will question me, and they cannot question the king until he awakes. We only need to get as far away as possible before that happens. Follow me."

They made their way through the courtyards and corridors of the palace. Whenever a servant stopped to ask Procne if everything was okay or if she needed any help, she told them a story about promising to let Itys see the dawn.

It all worked perfectly until they reached the main gate. Those guards were obviously more skeptical. They insisted that they would need to talk this over with the king. Procne didn't flinch.

"Oh, indeed, I do understand," Procne said with confidence. "But, you see, the king has drunk too much this evening. He is sleeping deeply at this very moment. If you, or one of your colleagues, would like to be the one to wake him from such a condition, I will not object. You must do what you must. Yet I insist you rush, for I do not want Prince Itys to sleep upright for much longer." Procne puffed out her cheeks in dramatic impatience while gently stroking Itys's hair. Zafira looked on, her face full of anxiety and impatience.

Three of the guards huddled up to mull over what they should do. Zafira found it funny that none of these big, beefy guards wanted to see puny little Tereus get upset.

They turned back toward Procne and agreed to let her go—*the bluff had worked!*—but…only if one guard came to stand watch while they slept.

Oh no!

Once again, Procne didn't even blink or hesitate. "Yes. That would be wise and very kind," the queen said. "I did not think to request something as crucial as protection through the night. We can never know what terrible monsters lurk outside our walls."

Procne nodded to the guard to lead on while leaning back toward Zafira and whispering, "If only he knew the REAL monster is inside the palace."

"But what are we going to do about him?" Zafira asked.

Procne nodded with a knowing expression and delicately handed Itys to Zafira. Zafira, who had never even touched a baby before, held him like a priceless vase, arms outstretched in front of her.

The young queen grabbed a thick tree branch from nearby, tip-toed up behind the guard, and clobbered him on the back of the head with unbelievable strength.

So much for being a dainty, delicate queen, Zafira smirked.

The guard fell forward with a groan but was conscious. He rubbed the back of his head and started cursing. Procne summoned whatever other fury she had repressed and slugged him again—really hard! This time it did the trick, and the guard slacked onto his side.

Procne leaned over him before gesturing for Zafira to get closer. "I hear his breathing. He will survive."

"I can't believe you hit him!" Zafira said, impressed, realizing it was the only way to buy them some time.

"Yes, well…it is done," Procne shrugged. "Now, come, Zafira! We need to put some distance between them and us. We must make haste—at once!"

CHAPTER 22: TOWERS AND CAVES

Procne grabbed all the long layers of her dress from behind, pulled them forward—and up, between her legs—and somehow tied them all together to make a kind of strange, poufy pair of shorts. She then scooped up her sleeping son and ran into the forest—gone in a flash.

Dude, that girl's quick when she means business.

Zafira took out the flashlight and sprinted to catch up. They were deep in the trees in no time.

Procne knew the way to the castle. So, with Zafira lighting the path—which Procne had proclaimed as 'pure magic'—they made it there lickety-split. They hid behind a tree near the front entrance. Zafira peeked out to study the tall stone structure.

It was dark and gloomy. Super creepy. It was also strangely narrow, giving the whole building a threatening, 'I'm-going-to-topple-over-and-crush-you' look. It had a flat roof with that unusual tower poking out one side.   Zafira shuddered at the looming, scary tower where Philomela was confined.

But she won't be a prisoner for much longer!

Itys, who had woken up during the forest dash, began to whimper. Procne soothed him to make sure his whimpers didn't turn into cries. Zafira decided to go ahead to see what the guard situation was like.

Only one guard was sitting on a stool near the entrance, and he was snoring—fast asleep. Zafira ran back to Procne and told her.

Procne smiled and turned to Itys. She whispered that he had to be quiet for the next few minutes while they played a funny game called 'Sleeping Guard.' Itys's eyes were droopy, but he nodded and smiled. Procne smoothed his hair and rubbed his cheeks like Zafira's mom often did.

Seconds later, the group made their move. It was the simplest sneak past so far. The guard didn't even twitch, and they easily slid through the unlocked entrance. Once inside, Zafira lit the way through dark, empty corridors and drafty, vacant courtyards. They found some narrow steps and climbed up to the tower.

In front of the tower doorway, there was an empty stool. Someone had likely once sat guard here, too.

But where is he now?

This was a bad sign.

The girls busted through the door. Zafira aimed the flashlight everywhere, but the room was empty.

"Oh no! Where is Philomela?" Procne called out. "Where is my sister?" Itys started to cry, and Procne quickly regrouped to calm him down.

Zafira scanned the large, square room. It had cold, stone walls and small, rectangular window openings near the ceiling. The whole thing felt like an ancient jail cell. It might have once had furniture, but it was completely empty now. Zafira grimaced at the harsh, cold place where Philomela had been imprisoned—for the second time since Zafira had met her.

Zafira soon came across a pile of wood in the corner. Something had been smashed to bits. Next to it, there was a bunched-up mound of material.

"What is this, Procne?" Zafira asked.

"That appears to be a broken weaving loom and…" Procne gathered the material with elation. "This is more of Philomela's weaving!"

"She left us another clue!" Zafira said, squealing and hugging Procne.

Together, they straightened out the cloth on the hard floor. Procne sat Itys down before kneeling to examine it closely and carefully. "The weaving is very unskillful and rushed," Procne said. "Clearly, my sister was in a hurry to finish."

"Does it show where she is? A place that you recognize?"

Procne nodded in slow motion. "Yes. It does, but oh—" She gasped. "It is too much! How much more are we to endure?"

"What does it show?" Zafira pleaded.

"Oh, Zafira," Procne rubbed her cheek with nervous energy. "She has woven an image of a cave—the cave below the king's palace. There are vast caverns below the cliffs, and I believe Tereus has taken Philomela into the depths below ground, where light and air do not flow freely, and monsters lurk without restraint!" Procne buried her face in Itys's neck.

Dark caves with monsters?

Zafira knew her dream was about to get even scarier.

***

138

They wasted no time in running down the steps and through the castle. Surprisingly, the main guard was still sleeping.

They scurried past him and into the dark forest.

At one point, they heard voices in the near distance. Zafira turned the flashlight off. They hid behind some overgrowth while five guards passed them, going toward the tower castle.

When the coast was clear, they sprinted the rest of the way to the edge of the forest and the cliffs beyond.

They zipped across the clearing, which was also unmanned, and Zafira worried that their luck was running out. At the edge, Procne pointed to a steep path that wound down toward a small, sandy beach by a round, little bay.

Zafira grunted. The descent would have been an unbelievably dangerous hike even on a bright, sunny day, let alone a dark, foggy night with guards on their heels. Still, she nodded and took the lead—both with her flashlight and her determination.

Zafira grinned at how strong she was in her dreams.

Too bad I'm not half as tough in real life, even though this all does feel so real!

Zafira scurried down the path, so consumed by the adventure and excitement that she couldn't believe it was a dream!

The moonlight reflecting off the sea helped light their way even more, and after several careful steps and slides, they made it to the beach. From there, they jogged a bit until they reached a cluster of large rocks. Zafira and Procne both held Itys's hands while they clambered over. There were a few more slips and scrapes, but they managed to get into the cool, pitch-black cave without serious injury.

Zafira turned to Procne. "Are you both okay?"

Procne was kneeling, smoothing out Itys's hair and

wiping his cheek. "The poor boy is terrified and tired. I keep telling him it is a game all young princes must play. Zafira, please reassure me it was not a mistake that I brought him with us? If anything were to happen to my—"

Zafira cut her off. "Don't worry, Procne. I still think Itys is safer with us than being with Tereus. I've got a flashlight, so the darkness isn't a problem. We'll run in here, get Philomela, and run back out. If you want, you guys can just wait for me?"

"No," Procne answered abruptly. "I am certain from now on we must all stay together—always. It may very well be our only weapon, our only strength."

Procne then turned toward the deep darkness and called out Philomela's name several times. There wasn't any response. "Oh, I hope we have not come here in error."

The girls trekked single-file down a narrow ledge along the left side of the cave. A large, black pool of water was to their right, several feet below. It was the tide from the sea.

Procne went first, carrying Itys in her arms, and Zafira followed right behind, shining the light ahead of them.

"See? This is easy," Zafira tried to sound calm. "No problem. One foot in front of the other. Just like—"

Suddenly, a large fish flew out of the water and hit Procne on the side of the head with its squirming tail. She tripped and was about to fall into the water with Itys when Zafira grabbed her by the arm. Procne used Zafira to regain her balance and steadied herself.

"What was that?" Procne asked, rubbing her head. She checked that Itys was fine. The boy whimpered and nodded.

Before they could think or say another word, the fish was back. This time though, it was flying toward Zafira.

Thankfully, Zafira's reflexes were still on, and she ducked to the left. The fish smacked into the cave wall. It fell down and slithered back into the water.

"It's some kind of angry flying fish or something," Zafira yelled.

Both girls were now facing the water. They were in position and ready to strike if the fish came out again.

Within seconds, the fish popped up again. But this time, it didn't fly or jump. It sort of 'stood up' on the water, supporting itself by its tail. When the girls realized what it was, they both screamed.

In reality, it was *half*-fish and half-scorpion—another hybrid! The creature's bottom half was all slimy and scaly, like a fish. But on top, it had a scorpion's head and pincers. It was over three feet long and was snapping its outstretched claws, threatening them.

Zafira had been right. Their luck had run out.

CHAPTER 23: ANGUISH AND ADVERSITY

"What do we do?" Procne yelled. She had turned her back to shield and protect Itys.

Zafira scoured the area. There wasn't anything to throw at it. Plus, it was too dark to aim well. She obviously couldn't jump on it since she'd be stabbed, chopped up, or drowned. And that would be a one-way ticket back to Davis with no final conclusion.

So, what now?

Zafira thought about luring it away. "Run, Procne!" Zafira yelled over her shoulder while running back out of the cave. Procne understood and bolted in the opposite direction, going further inside.

"Okay, you ugly fish-thing, you...come and get me!" Zafira shrieked.

Apparently, the fish creature wasn't as stupid or predictable as Zafira had hoped. Instead, it turned toward Procne, dipped underwater, and flew out—right at her.

Zafira screamed and sprinted back toward Procne.

Luckily, Zafira's scream caught Procne's attention, and

she stopped just in time. The predator fish misjudged its leap and hit the cave wall inches in front of Procne's nose. It landed hard on the edge of the ledge and squirmed back underwater.

Zafira caught up to them. "I'm sorry. I was trying to get it to chase me," she said, panting.

"We have to get off this narrow path at once," Procne said while rocking Itys. "Do you believe the way will open up further inside?"

"I hope so!" Zafira noticed the water moving again. "Go, Procne! It's coming!"

The girls raced off. But they couldn't run *too* fast so as not to trip and fall into the water. Plus, they could barely see because they were deep inside the darkness; the moonlight was fading, and Zafira's bobbing flashlight wasn't enough.

Zafira heard the scary sound of swirling, gurgling water before something yanked her ponytail backward. She yelped. A sharp pain radiated to her scalp.

"It's got me by the hair!" Zafira cried out.

Without hesitation and with all her might, Zafira bit her lip and whipped her head around like a choreographed dance move. She smacked the fish creature against the cave wall. Its scorpion-like pincers lost their grip, and it fell into the seawater again.

"Arghhh! You stupid creature!!!" Zafira yelled at it and rubbed the back of her head.

Just then, Procne pointed to some bumpy forms ahead.

"Zafira! In the distance…your light…there…do you see? Stalagmites! Oh, yes…and the water appears to be less deep. We are getting closer to—"

But Procne couldn't finish. The fish creature was back.

Suddenly, Itys let out a giant howl. The sound reverberated and echoed throughout the cave. Itys had been crying the entire time, but these new wails were much louder and more intense.

"Is he hurt?" Zafira asked.

"He is fine," Procne replied. "Only terrified."

But something happened. The fish creature reared up and immediately retreated underwater. It circled back again to peek out at Itys. Its claws were motionless. The creature seemed dazed and hesitant.

When Itys saw the disgusting water creature, he sobbed even louder and clawed at his mother's neck, trying to escape.

As soon as it heard the louder cries, the fish creature reeled back, dove under the water, and swam away. It left some ripples on the water's surface and then was gone.

"It didn't like Itys's cries!" Zafira said. She aimed the flashlight all over the pool, but nothing remained. "Maybe it got scared or bothered by the echoes! Good job, Itys!"

Zafira rubbed the child's back. Procne continued to nuzzle, soothe, and calm him. "But let's not wait around to make sure," Procne stated.

They tottered the last few steps toward the clearing and jumped off the ledge in front of the stalagmites. The trio delicately maneuvered over the sharp and jagged cave formations. By helping each other along, they got past the pointy obstacles and made it back onto flat, dry land. There were a few puddles, or tiny pools, here and there, but they got around those with no trouble.

They rushed forward in silence—the only words were Procne's calls to her sister. It took ten or so times until they heard something at last. In the dark distance, there was an unmistakable groan and whine.

Zafira and Procne screamed joyfully, hugged each other, and kissed Itys. "Philomela!" Zafira called out. "It's Zafira,

Procne, and Itys! We're all here! We're coming! We're coming to get you! Hold on!"

The girls pushed on—faster and faster. Now, they were almost jogging forward, floating along on their relief. As they went further, the boggy areas and small pools got bigger and bigger. Finally, they reached an enormous pond.

Zafira flashed the light on both sides. They wouldn't be able to go around this one. This time, they'd have to cross through it.

"Let me try first," Zafira offered. She shuffled into the water. It was cool and fresh. She shivered a little, but it wasn't too deep. It came up below her knees. She waded all the way across to see if any sections got deeper. When Zafira was sure it was safe and shallow enough, she walked back over to help Procne and Itys.

After that pond, there was another wide pool a couple feet ahead. "Truly, I hope these pools of water will not become bigger and deeper as we near Philomela," Procne said.

"Don't worry! They'll probably all be like the last one," Zafira replied. She didn't even hesitate to step in first. But the second her sneakered foot touched the water, she screamed and pulled back.

"It's boiling!" She shrieked and fell to the ground.

Zafira gawked at the rubber-soled running shoe that had saved her foot. She touched the bottom and snatched her fingers away. "It's still hot!"

"How is that possible?" Procne asked. "There are no bubbles, no vapors!"

Zafira tested the water by dipping the tip of the flashlight's metal handle inside. She left it in only a few seconds and then touched the bottom with her finger again.

"Ow! Feel that! It's burning!"

Zafira let Procne test it. The young queen hesitated but then aimed her pinky finger at the hot metal. She yanked it away when she felt the heat.

After blowing on the flashlight to cool it back down, Zafira turned it on to scan the middle of the pool. From there, they could now clearly see the steam rising from the water. It must have been scorching.

"Great," Zafira yelled out sarcastically. "Now this? What'll be next? Three-headed creatures? Angry lions? Can't we just get there already?" Zafira huffed with impatience.

Procne paced nearby with Itys in her arms, her face full of worry and defeat.

Zafira stared at the boiling pond, treading along its edge. Feeling discouraged, she kicked a small rock into the hot water and watched it disappear.

Then, she broke off a long, thin stalagmite near the cave wall and dipped it into the water. She prodded at the hot pool for a second, seeing it was even shallower than the first one they had crossed.

Seems about ankle-high.

Zafira shined the light across to the far edge of the pool, where she saw a large, long log. She scoffed.

And that's how the little weasel got over the first time with Philomela and probably how he got back out again on his own.

But Zafira couldn't figure out how Tereus was strong enough to throw that log back over to the other side when he was done. Zafira growled and felt her skin crawl with hatred.

Zafira glared stubbornly at the pool. *It really isn't that far—*

Instantly, she made a decision. Zafira dropped her bag, bent down to take off her shoes and socks, and rolled her jeans to her knees.

"Zafira? Zafira? What are you thinking?" Procne asked, her voice laced with fear.

Zafira didn't answer. In the worst-case scenario, she'd be burned to 'dream death' and wake up. Then she'd have to hope and wait to return to these girls again.

But maybe, just maybe, this could work...

Zafira took a deep breath, held it, and high-kneed right into the boiling pond. The entire five seconds it took her to cross, Zafira channeled visions from documentaries she had seen with her parents where people had walked over hot coals or gone swimming in frozen lakes. Like what happened with the vine creature, she could *feel* pain in this dream. But focusing on something besides the pain helped her.

And just like that, she did it. She sprang and bounded her way safely to the other side.

When she got there, she spun around in a daze. Then she grinned across to Procne. "I'm okay!" Zafira pointed to her beet-red feet. "It looks worse than it feels. I'm red and sore—kind of like a really bad sunburn—but, honestly, it's okay!"

"Oh, Zafira, why did you do something so foolish?"

Zafira gave a thumbs up. "Don't worry, Procne. It's all good! Now hold on while I push that log into place, so you both can get over."

It took Zafira a few minutes to pull, drag, and push the heavy log into and across the pool. Once she had, she strode back over to get Procne, Itys, and her stuff.

Procne squeezed her tight, smooshing Itys in between them. Itys had stopped crying. Apparently, seeing a crazy girl jumping through boiling hot water was enough to shock and confuse the crying out of him.

Procne ran back to the last pool and, using Zafira's

bottle, retrieved some cool water to pour onto Zafira's scalded feet. Minutes later, Zafira had gradually slipped her shoes and socks on again, and the group crossed over the bumpy log.

They passed two more wide pools. But miraculously, these were like the earlier ones: cool and fresh. They were easy to pass, and Zafira made sure to go through each barefoot. The cool water was heavenly soothing. Zafira still couldn't believe how physically real both pain and relief were in this dream!

After every pond, Procne continued to call out to Philomela. They were reassured by every grunt or groan, but why wasn't she *saying* anything?

Is she gagged?

Zafira felt her stomach lurch at the thought of her poor friend suffering even more.

At the next pool, Zafira bent down to take off her shoes again. "Oh no!" she cried, flashing the light on the moving water. "There's something in this one!"

CHAPTER 24: JOY AND PAIN

This pond had more than just *one* thing, though. It was full of small, glittery, snake-like fish—eels. But when Zafira got closer, she also discovered blobs that appeared to be tiny, glowing jellyfish. The whole body of water pulsed and shimmered.

"Arghh!" Zafira grimaced at the slithering forms.

"Oh, Zafira," Procne said, making an 'ewww' sound. "I have been told about these water creatures. They can shock and kill!"

"Oh, you're right! They're electric!" Zafira grumbled. "That's why the water looks like it's glowing!"

"Electric?"

"It's something dangerous," Zafira replied simply. "It means that the whole pool is full of something that humans can't touch, especially not in water. There's absolutely no way to go in there!"

Procne sighed with exasperation and cradled Itys. She patrolled the entire edge of the pond, bouncing Itys with every step. Zafira shadowed them, scanning the sides of the cave for any solution.

Zafira racked her brain for her science class memories, trying to remember if jellyfish were found in oceans and seas while eels were only found in rivers.

Or is it the other way around? And can they even co-exist?

Zafira rubbed her jaw, lost in thought. She had definitely seen jellyfish in the sea in Greece, but maybe those were different? Zafira paced and pondered.

"Well, Tereus must have passed this somehow, like he did with the log before." Zafira shined the light around the pool.

"Over there!" Procne exclaimed, pointing to the left side of the pond, where the water met the cave wall.

Zafira ran over and found several jagged, irregular pieces of rock jutting from the wall.

"That jerk!" Zafira yelled. "He probably used those rocks to get over with Philomela, but he must have smashed them after using each one to get back out. Arrggghhh! I can't believe it! Can't stand that guy!"

And just seconds after her courageous crossing, Zafira's frustration and despair were back. Add to that her building impatience and ongoing confusion, and Zafira was about ready to throw in the towel. She was in desperate need of her cave time. What she wouldn't give to be surrounded by her pillows, under her covers, in her dark bedroom.

How ironic that I need my cave time from this cave time! Zafira snorted.

Zafira plopped down on the side of the pool and stared at its mesmerizing glow. All she had wanted was a simple escape—a dream passage into a world full of adventure and intrigue. She sure got that.

But I also got one problem after another. Zafira huffed in frustration.

And yet...there was more; a lot more, like exciting sights, strange challenges, and new experiences. But the best part was that Zafira got to see what was important to two girls from three thousand years ago, which was simple: love, family, and friendship.

Suddenly, Zafira knew precisely why she was there...and she had an idea of what to do.

Zafira bent over the edge of the pool and started making spit. At first, it was tiny spittle, then mouthfuls of saliva, and finally, using every muscle in her mouth and jaw, she worked up a huge glob of spit and let loose.

Nothing happened at first. But then, steadily, the water changed color. It became darker and murkier.

"Something is happening!" Procne exclaimed with delight.

Zafira's eyes got wider, and she could have sworn the whole cave let out a sigh of relief.

Zafira went on making and spewing spit. She did it five times until all she had left in her mouth was hot air and dust.

Then it was time to check. Zafira decided to give it a try by sticking her pinky in. "It can't be worse than sticking your finger in a socket, and I did that once when I was five," Zafira said. "It was scary, and I got a shock, but I'm still alive."

Procne, who was completely confused, just smiled and nodded. Zafira took a few deep breaths and went for it. She dipped her left pinky halfway into the top of the water. As soon as it touched, she knew it had worked.

"But how did you know?" Procne asked, perplexed.

"I mean, my spit worked like magic before, and I thought, well, we don't have anything to lose." Zafira shrugged and smiled, not adding that sometimes solutions came clearly in her dreams. Just like that. And not just for dream problems. But also life problems. Yaya had always loved the old saying: 'Sleep on it,' and often reminded Zafira to do just that when she couldn't figure out an answer to a problem.

Zafira went across the pond first. After that, Procne carried Itys up on her shoulders, gripping him by the legs. They had finally reached the other side—safe, wet, and exhausted.

Then, they were on the move again.

"Quick," Zafira said with intensity. "The cave turns to the left up ahead. I think we're probably close."

The group sloshed onward. After the turn, the cave narrowed into a small, low passageway.

"Philomela?" Zafira called out into the darkness.

"Mmmhhhmm!!" The cry was loud and close.

"Philomela, if that's you, can you please say something? Or just come to us?" Zafira pleaded. She shined the light as far as possible but couldn't see the end of the cave.

"Mmmmhhhhmmmmmm!!" The same cry, only longer and more emphatic.

Something must definitely be covering her mouth.

"Don't worry, we'll come to you." Zafira turned to Procne. "Okay, time to save your sister."

The girls scurried the last few feet to get to Philomela's shadowy form at the back end of the cave. But when they got close enough, they both gasped.

Philomela was tied up, hunched over, and emaciated. Her frail, skinny body floated underneath an old, rough, brown sack of a dress. Her hair was a bramble of knots and clumps. Her eyes were sunken in, rimmed with gray shadows. She looked like she hadn't eaten or drunk anything in days. But the worst part was that she wasn't gagged, and nothing covered her mouth.

Both Zafira and Procne wondered the same thing at the same time: *Why hasn't she said anything?*

They soon found out because when Philomela opened her mouth to groan again, they saw...nothing. Between her teeth was a dark, black, gaping void where her tongue should have been.

"Philomela!" Procne screamed.

"Philomela! Your tongue! What happened to your tongue?" Zafira cried out.

Philomela sobbed, moaned, gagged, and made every other inarticulate noise possible—every noise but speech. Both Zafira and Procne, who was still holding Itys, collapsed beside her, wrapping her up in a group hug. Everyone was crying.

Zafira pulled away first. She hurried to untie Philomela's hands from her feet and her feet from the stake. Zafira wished she had some fresh water to give her, but they didn't. The young princess then tottered up and fell onto her sister. They both kept sobbing and grasping onto their gowns—as if they were tethering themselves to each other so neither one could fly away.

"Sister! Dear sister! He told me you were dead! I can't...I can't..." Procne's powerful sobs gagged her, too.

Zafira took a deep breath, swallowing back her own tears, and knew she'd have to do the talking. "Philomela, is it true? Is your tongue really gone?"

Philomela nodded, grabbed Zafira's hand, and buried her cheek. Zafira felt the hot tears on her palm.

"Did Tereus do this to you?" Zafira continued.

Another nod. Another sob.

Procne cried out again, and Philomela turned toward her sister. When Procne faced her sister's anguish, Procne buried her head into Itys neck. Philomela hugged them both before standing back to get a good look at her nephew for the first time.

"Philo, this is my son, Itys," Procne said gently. "He has heard many beautiful stories of you." Procne then whispered to her son. "Give your Thea Philomela a warm hug, my prince."

Itys slowly leaned over from his mom's embrace to cradle Philomela's neck. The little group was a ball of tears, smiles, and hugs.

Zafira loved the reunion but remembered Tereus would likely still have people out looking for Procne and Itys. Plus, Philomela was dehydrated. They needed to get out of there as soon as possible.

"Do you think you can walk?" Zafira asked the princess. "We have to get outta here…fast."

Philomela rubbed the sore skin around her ankles—where she had been bound—and nodded. Fortunately, Tereus had at least left her sandals.

Philomela mouthed: "I am ready." And with that, they all turned to go.

Zafira led the way with the flashlight, Philomela in the middle, and Procne—with Itys piggyback—in the rear.

They managed to get out most of Philomela's story along the way by playing a sad version of the Yes/No game. Zafira would ask 'Yes' or 'No' questions, and the princess would grunt either once, for yes, or twice, for no.

They discovered that Philomela had willingly come with Tereus to be reunited with her sister. At first, Philomela was so happy and excited. But on the boat trip, in a crazy rage, Tereus attacked her and later cut out her tongue so she wouldn't be able to tell anyone what had happened. Philomela had passed out from the pain and woke in the tower castle.

Suddenly, Zafira recalled something from before. "But I remember your tongue was already bothering you when we were together last time," Zafira said, shocked.

Philomela shrugged sadly.

"I guess it was all some freaky warning we couldn't understand," Zafira said, looking down with sadness and guiding them through the pools. They had already passed the electric one—the creatures were still neutralized—and crossed the boiling pond on the log.

Philomela's sad story continued. When she had woke up in the tower castle, she had tried to starve herself, but they forced her food and water. Tereus even had the servants bring her weaving materials as a joke—a cruel reminder of her simple, peaceful life from before.

But that was his crucial mistake because Philomela had already become friends with one of the servants who helped her get her message out. Still, Tereus had suspected that friendship, so he had Philomela moved to the caves just days earlier.

By the time Philomela finished grunting her last reply, Procne's sniffles were still echoing off the cave walls. "This suffering, I see now, was all because he would have preferred to marry you," Procne said. "But I was the elder, and so there was no choice. Yet now, I understand. If he could not have you, then no man would. And he attacked you out of jealousy. Oh, what a wretched, terrible man! I am so...so sorry! Dear Philomela, what horrors you have had to endure!" Procne exploded into sobs again, and the group had to stop walking to console her.

A few minutes later, they were on the move again. They had rushed through most of the harmless ponds and were almost out. The moonlight was beckoning them ahead, but there was still that first lagoon.

As they got closer to the exit, Procne spoke up once more. "I do not know what additional horrors await us outside this cave, but I know that I am ready to die if I need to…to protect my sister, my son, and my new friend."

"Procne!" Zafira protested.

"No," Procne said firmly. "It is true, Zafira. I do not *want* to die, but I would if I could save any of you. Indeed, I feel that what Philomela has had to suffer was a fault of mine. I will not let it happen again. If there is any way I can remove or change the damage that my wretched matrimony has caused, I will live my entire life in hopes of achieving that."

Procne faced the last pool by the entrance. They didn't know if the fish creature would attack, but they were ready to find out.

Procne turned to her sister, cupped her face, and said, "You are still the most beautiful woman in the world! I will do everything to protect you from now on. We will escape and return to our beloved home in Athens, where you will rest and recover in every way. Then, we will begin to live again and forget this agony!" Procne hugged her, and Philomela embraced both her sister and her nephew.

"Okay, girls, but first, we've got to see if this crazy fish thing is still here," Zafira said, looking at the murky water for any movement. Luckily, there wasn't any.

"I think we should just make a run for it," Zafira whispered.

The girls agreed, and they zipped down the length of the ledge and made it out safely into the pre-dawn darkness. They each collapsed to the ground, exhausted and in need of rest.

But there wasn't any time. A line of guards was coming toward them.

CHAPTER 25: PREPARATIONS
AND PREDICTIONS

"They are coming!" Procne whispered and pointed. The soldiers were clambering over the same rocks Zafira and Procne had climbed earlier.

"We will be found," Procne added. "Quick! We must hide! But where?" The queen shushed and rocked Itys.

Zafira frantically scanned the beach. The guards were approaching fast. But at least it was still dark, and her flashlight was off. They probably hadn't seen them yet, but where could the girls hide? There wasn't anything taller than a rock in front of them.

Behind them, to the left of the cave entrance, a series of rocks and boulders were just wide enough for them to squeeze behind. There wasn't time to wonder. Zafira tugged at the sisters and led the way.

They silently maneuvered over to the rocky corner. One by one, they scrunched between the cave wall and the rocks. Procne went in first with Itys, ensuring he was comfortable enough not to cry. Next, Philomela shimmied in, followed by Zafira, who had to twist and contort herself to find the last bit of cover.

Zafira's scalp stuck out, but the guards were steps away, so all she did was close her eyes and hope that her invisibility hadn't worn off or that none of them veered even a little to the left. As the guards got closer, the hidden group held their collective breath.

"Follow closely, men." This came from the leading guard. Then from some grumbling, mumbling soldiers in the back, they heard:

"Ah, we have to go in there?"

"Silly woman, that Queen!"

"I hate caves."

"Truly, did we need to wake so early for this foolish search?"

Soon, the voices and footsteps faded. Zafira risked it and peeked over the top of the rock. There was no one around.

She poked Philomela, who pulled at Procne, and the four of them carefully spilled out of their hiding spot. They were scratched, wet, sandy, and cold, but they nodded to each other and ran toward the path.

They made it over the rocks and were dashing down the length of the sandy beach when Zafira yanked them both back. Up ahead, one stray soldier was guarding the entrance to the path.

Obviously, they would have left one guard back to watch the path. Zafira groaned.

But Procne was on the move again. Maybe she was inspired by her last successful attempt at knocking out a guard. Or maybe she was motivated by her new determination to help and protect the rest of them. For whatever reason, Procne simply handed Itys to Philomela and marched faced-on to the guard.

Ironically, the guard was caught off-guard when the queen appeared before him. His mouth dropped, and he didn't even have a second to wield his sword before Procne attacked.

She let out a savage growl, and, like a ferocious, rabid squirrel, she went right for his eyes. Zafira was shocked, and Philomela stood motionless while Procne viciously clawed and scratched at the guard.

He yelled and screamed and swatted at Procne. "Help me!" Procne roared, snapping them out of their trance.

They reacted like trained warriors. Zafira wrestled his sword out of his grasp and tossed it as far away as possible. Meanwhile, Philomela set Itys down, grabbed a nearby rock, and smashed it onto the side of his head.

The guard was clearly outmatched by their unified ferocity. He passed out, falling limply to the ground. A small trickle of blood dribbled from his left temple, but he was still breathing. He would survive, but was the same true for them?

"The other guards probably heard his scream, so we've got to get up there fast!" Zafira yelled.

Procne and Philomela went first. Even with occasional switchbacks and diagonals, the narrow path was brutal to climb. Within minutes, the girls had slowed down from running to jogging to barely staggering.

The climb was especially hard for Procne, who had to carry Itys. It was also grueling for Philomela, who was so thin and weak, she could hardly stand. But they somehow dug deep into some pit of inner strength and huffed and puffed their way to the top.

"We're lucky there's no guard up here, but we're still not safe." Zafira bent over, heaving. Once again, her physical pain was so real, so genuine, she couldn't believe she was in a dream!

Zafira swallowed hard and added, "I think we should hide out in the thickest part of the forest until we can regroup. Is that okay?"

Both Procne and Philomela nodded. Procne led the way. She took them first west along the cliffs, and when she was satisfied they were far enough away from the palace, she pointed into the dense, wooded area to the north.

They took turns sprinting across the exposed hundred and fifty yards between the edge of the cliffs and the forest's tree line, making it into the cool, protected cover of the trees in a flash.

"Now, you must stay behind me carefully," Procne whispered, still out of breath. "This forest has several different types of trees. I believe our best hope for hiding is not up high—in the branches. But rather inside one of the trees."

"Inside?" Zafira asked, wiping the sweat from her eyes.

"Yes," Procne added. "There are many large, old trees in this forest. Indeed, many of them have big open areas you can crawl into. Certainly, we can find a group of them where we will all be safe and hidden."

"Oh! Tree hollows!" Zafira said, nodding. So, using Zafira's flashlight, they headed deep into the forest.

Philomela had the insight to use a piece of thread from Procne's shawl to tie around the branches of the trees as they passed. Philomela made sure to climb up higher than the height of an adult male and tied them tightly around the branches. The thread was invisible to the eye—except for someone who knew where to look...someone who would use this to find their way back out.

Zafira was impressed with Philomela's *Hansel and Gretel*

solution. Plus, it instantly reminded her of the story of Ariadne, the Minotaur, and Theseus.

Is this what Yaya means about my subconscious acting up again? Well, either way, I've got hours of stuff to tell Yaya! And to write about in my journal!

But first, Zafira had to see how this dream would end.

When they got deep enough, Procne found two large hollows and gathered leaves and sticks with Philomela's help to make as soft a cradle as possible for Itys and themselves. Zafira found a big enough hollow a few trees away.

But, just as she was peering into the massive hole of twisted wood and roots, something flew right at her.

Zafira screamed and covered her face. From the crook of her elbow, she heard and felt fluttering wings. She stepped back. It was an owl. As soon as she unblocked the hollow, the small bird flew away.

The others came running up. "What happened?" Procne asked.

"I'm so sorry. I shouldn't have yelled. It was an owl," Zafira answered. "It scared me, that's all. Do you think anyone heard?"

"No," Procne said. "We are well ahead of the guards and quite deep in the forest. I have not heard anything behind us, so I believe we are safe. However, we must be cautious and quiet." Procne unfurrowed her brows and grinned. "Ah, but Zafira, the owl is an excellent omen. It is Athena's companion."

Zafira thought back to her dream journal. *Who knew the owl on there was good luck!*

She smiled and turned to Philomela, who was also grinning. "I see you smiling, Philomela," Zafira said with a chuckle. "I know what you're thinking: Athena's helping us."

Philomela's grin broadened.

"Well, I don't know about all that," Zafira replied, smiling back. "All I know is there goes *another* bird out here! You guys and your birds! Sheesh!"

"Yes, well, hopefully, Athena is on our side," Procne added. "Today, we are tired and should rest and—" she was interrupted by a loud stomach growl coming from Itys. Procne rubbed his belly before continuing. "We are also hungry and thirsty, and I will soon fetch us food and water."

"Oh, but Procne, let me do it," Zafira added. "It'll be much easier for me; that way, you can stay here with Itys and Philomela."

Procne seemed like she was about to protest but nodded reluctantly instead. "It is true, Zafira; your invisibility will be an asset once more. I thank you for offering." She cleared her throat and went on. "But then later tonight, with darkness as our strength, we will return to the palace and attack."

"But how are we supposed to attack Tereus with all his guards?" Zafira asked.

"Do not forget, Zafira, I am the queen, and that sleeping boy back there is the prince. The guards will not dare touch me. At most, they will merely bring us to Tereus, which is what we want. For when I am in front of that monster, I will finish him before anyone else can react. When there is no more Tereus, the guards will have no choice but to be loyal to the prince and me."

Zafira just hoped everything would work. But her subconscious knew better.

***

Zafira followed the thread back out of the forest. It was

much quicker this way. She was out in no time, realizing they might not be as deep as they had assumed.

Zafira raced out. She piled some branches and leaves so she'd know where to turn back in and then ran toward the palace. She followed the cliffs, keeping the sea to her right.

Amazingly, there weren't any guards to be seen. Zafira hoped that meant they were either reconvening back in the palace or looking in the wrong part of the forest.

At the front gate, Zafira snuck by the few guards on patrol. She zigzagged her way back to one of the storerooms. Zafira filled her bag with whatever she could grab: different types of fruit, vegetables, some bread, and nuts. She then filled her water bottle and another deep *rhyton* with water from a large container, which she hid under her sweatshirt. The hardest part was trying not to spill.

Zafira was back out into the colorful corridors of the palace within minutes. All of a sudden, she heard a distinctive sticky voice behind her. Her stomach lurched.

Zafira turned around in slow motion and saw Tereus talking to a guard. The guard was almost three heads taller than the puny king.

"That is fine," Tereus said. "Keep searching the forest. Expand the area. Are we certain they are not still on the beach or in the cave?"

"Yes, my king," the guard replied. "My men meticulously searched both areas. The stake was where you said it would be, but indeed, it was empty. So, they must have retrieved the prisoner before we arrived. They must have also hid on the beach when we passed and attacked the one soldier before escaping up the hill and into the forest."

"And, this soldier, the one they attacked, he is well?' Tereus inquired.

"Yes, my king. He was already awake when we arrived.

His head was slightly bruised, but he will be fine."

"No, he will not! Immediately, I order you to kill him," Tereus spewed cruelly. Zafira gasped and shivered, which made her drip some water. Luckily, no one noticed.

"Do you understand?" Tereus went on. "This is an order. You must kill that worthless guard. Is that clear?"

The guard hesitated for a few seconds before nodding once and leaving.

"Have no doubt," Tereus called after him.

The guard stopped and turned back to face the king.

"She will return here," Tereus said. "Sooner or later, my silly, selfish queen will come crawling back to me. She cannot take care of herself or anyone. She will not escape. She will never escape!"

Tereus then waved the soldier away and turned around. The tiny tyrant marched by Zafira, passed through an open courtyard, and disappeared around a corner.

Zafira rolled her eyes before spinning around and making her way slowly back out past the guards. She soon reached the tree with her strange pile of branches. She turned into the forest and followed the thread back to the girls. Zafira found Philomela resting beside Procne and Itys's tree hollow. The girls were holding hands while they slept.

Zafira didn't want to wake them, but she knew they needed to eat. So, she gently shook Philomela, who woke up with a flinch and a grunt. Philomela smiled with relief when she saw Zafira. Procne also woke up and nudged Itys awake. Zafira sat down next to them.

"Well, girls, I have good news and bad news," Zafira said as she passed around the food and water. Zafira and Philomela shared the water bottle, while Procne and Itys drank from the *rhyton*.

"What is 'news'?" Procne asked while feeding Itys a soft fig.

"Oh, yeah...sorry. I mean, I have good and bad information to tell you."

Philomela waved her on with her hand while devouring a plum.

"The guards are searching the forest, but much further down," Zafira said. Both sisters sighed.

Zafira turned to face Procne. "But Tereus knows you'll be coming back to the palace. He said some mean things about you, but basically, the important thing is...he'll be waiting for us."

Procne's jaw tightened, and she glared off into the distance. "Let him wait, for he will *not* be ready for the woman coming back for him."

CHAPTER 26: HOPES AND DREAMS

The girls finished eating and drinking in silence—each lost in thought. Procne had tried putting Itys back to sleep, but the boy still stirred. He was obviously too scared to sleep.

Because, really, what kid could sleep after all we've been through?

So, Zafira distracted him with stories about cars, trains, and planes.

Itys was enthralled, especially with the idea of flying.

"Mama, when I old, I fly?" the young child asked, innocent and sweet.

"Ah, my little one, I think we will have to keep flying only in our dreams," Procne chuckled and snuggled her son.

This sparked Zafira's curiosity. "Hey girls, so after we beat Tereus, which we *will* do, what will you two do next?"

Philomela jumped up, snapped her fingers, and did a little jig.

Zafira understood right away. "Yup, I think dancing and celebrating will definitely be in order," Zafira said and laughed. "Procne, how about you?"

"Oh, but my dear, Zafira, it is almost too much to believe. I will be so overjoyed to be free of my treacherous husband." Procne combed her fingers through Itys's hair. She was silent for a moment, and then she went on to describe how sad she had been since she got married.

Not only because Tereus was so disgusting and horrible and because Procne thought Philomela had died. But also because it had felt like there was nothing else to look forward to. Procne added that life had gotten a little better when Itys was born, but it had always been a bittersweet combination of joy and fear, especially fear that he would grow more like his father.

"But now...now..." Procne's face lit up. "Now I am here with my sister *and* my son! I am full of love and happiness again. I do not know what will happen tonight, but I fear no more. I feel free for the first time since I was a child. What else could I want or yearn for?"

Philomela reached over and squeezed her sister's hand.

"That's great," Zafira said, drawing out the word, "But now you can let yourself dream of something more, something bigger...something that will always bring you happiness."

"Certainly, when we return to Athens, I will beg my father—after all we have been through—to allow us both time to heal, and Itys as well, before he finds us both husbands," Procne replied.

"Husbands?" Zafira almost choked on her bread. "But that's not what I'm talking about. I mean, like, what will you *do*?"

Procne seemed confused. "Zafira, but what do you mean? Do? There is nothing to do. We will be married; of that, there is no choice. Our father is the king and needs to marry off all his children. Not only for the continuation of the royal family line but because it is what is required in our society."

Philomela nodded slowly.

Zafira looked down. *I guess that's just how it is back here.*

She felt sad for a bit but saw their smiles and relaxed. It was comforting to Zafira to think that they'd be happy in their own way—a way that made sense with their lives here, even if it made no sense in her own.

"Perhaps, this time, I will have a husband who will not be so cruel," Procne added. "Yes, I will wish for that…and a good upbringing for my son, who one day will become a great ruler himself."

Procne sighed and took one more sip of water. "But, girls, we must rest," she said in her motherly tone. "Zafira, I thank you so much for your lovely stories. Now, run off to your tree, and please, try to sleep."

Of course, Zafira knew she wouldn't be able to sleep in her dream, but she went off and let the sisters try to rest anyway.

***

That evening, after finishing off the leftover fruit, bread, and water from before, they followed the threads back out of the forest. They came out just as dusk was turning to night and made straight for the palace.

Procne was in the middle, carrying Itys on her back, with Zafira on the left and Philomela on the right. No one said a word. They simply marched in one tight, unified line.

Two guards recognized them as they approached the palace and rushed to detain them. Zafira was still invisible, so she followed along behind.

While the guards were binding their hands behind her

back, Procne spoke in a calm, steady voice.

"Guards, you know very well that I am Queen Procne, first daughter of King Pandion of the great city of Athens and wife to King Tereus. This is Prince Itys, and this other woman is Princess Philomela, second daughter to King Pandion—left for dead in the caves below. You will treat us with the care and respect that royal persons require, and I demand that you take us directly to King Tereus."

The guards were silent. They grabbed them firmly, pried Itys away from Procne, surrounded them, and led them through the corridors and courtyards of the palace. At one point, Zafira ran up behind both girls to loosen their rope ties.

The group shuffled through a porch-like entrance into an enormous room in the center of the palace. Tereus sat on a tall chair, waiting for them like he said he would. And they came right to him like he said they would!

Zafira wanted to punch something—preferably Tereus's face. At least he looked ridiculous in that chair that was too big and too tall for him. He was like a little kid in his highchair.

The swanky room had a very high ceiling supported by several columns, which separated an inner square section from a large outer area. Colorful, tiny tiles lined the floor, paintings decorated the walls, and there were flashy, clashing patterns all around.

Tereus's throne was on the right wall, making it the first thing people saw when they entered the massive room. In the back corner was another smaller doorway, which Zafira noticed led to a storeroom of some kind. She wondered if that led out somewhere.

An escape?

"Welcome to my *megaron*, Philomela," Tereus said, all

phlegmy and creepy. The miniature king clasped his hands together, breaking out into the most disturbing, sinister grin.

Tereus turned to one of the soldiers and said, "I require merely two guards. The rest, leave now. Return to your duties."

After the guards dispersed, only two were left, holding on to Procne and Philomela. Itys stood frightened behind one of the interior columns, and Tereus motioned him to come over. The boy hesitated, and when Tereus saw his reluctance, he yelled, "Get over here…NOW!"

Itys ran over to him, trembling. Procne bit her lip. Zafira knew she was straining to keep from lashing out.

Zafira walked by one of the wall paintings. It showed a tall, muscular Tereus standing proudly at the front of a ship, being rowed by hundreds of men. It was unrealistic in every way. And not just fake Tereus, but even the boat seemed to float awkwardly in the middle of the two-dimensional waves. Around the painting, Zafira saw simple sketches of fish, dolphins, and other sea creatures. It reminded her of some images in one of Yaya's art history books.

Of course, the little runt would have someone paint him looking tall and strong.

Zafira shook her head. She turned back toward the girls and was happy to see that Philomela already had her hands free and was only holding on to the ropes for appearances.

Meanwhile, Tereus went on spewing. "It is a pleasure to see you again, my queen…and with your beautiful sister." He stiffly patted the top of Itys's head. "Yes, very, very nice. You see, we are all together…one happy family."

Tereus turned toward one of the guards and said, "Thank you, guards. Thank you for protecting my possessions." He put extra stress on the last word.

Zafira scanned the room for something she could throw

at him.

Let's see how he likes being whacked by one of his possessions! It was taking all her strength to stay calm and invisible.

Tereus then got up ungracefully from his throne and approached the girls. He was as tall as Philomela and a smidge shorter than Procne. He sauntered around them, and Philomela hastily but believably repositioned the rope.

Procne couldn't hold it in another second. "I have only contempt for what you have done to my sister, to me, to my family...to all of us." She articulated every slow, deliberate word, keeping her eyes on Itys the entire time. "I have come here to tell you we are leaving immediately. And to warn you that when King Pandion hears of this, you will be hunted and killed for your crimes."

Tereus let out a squeaky laugh. Zafira grimaced. It reminded her of a scary clown she had seen at a circus years ago.

"You came to tell me what? What was that again? You are leaving? YOU?" He continued to laugh.

Procne stayed calm and firm. "Yes. Immediately. Now, command your men to release us and allow me the time to organize my things and those of Itys. If you wish to be of assistance, you could arrange our sea transport. Perhaps my father may spare your life if he hears that you acted rationally in these matters."

Tereus kept laughing and pacing. "Indeed, I always knew you were a stupid woman, nowhere near as intelligent or beautiful as your sister. Yet, this is a new level of ignorance. Do you really think I will merely release you both?"

Procne swallowed hard and replied, "Yes."

"Well...you are...CORRECT!" Tereus smiled.

Both sisters, plus an invisible Zafira, turned in shock at

the little monster of a man.

"What? Does that surprise you?" Tereus asked with a few tsks. "You surely do not know your own husband, my queen. Here, let me begin by helping the guards do exactly that—release you."

When he gurgled out the last two words, Tereus pranced to one of the guards and demanded his sword. The guard bowed obediently and handed the king his bronze inlaid sword.

As soon as Tereus wielded the sword, he slid the blade into the bowing soldier's side without hesitation. The guard flopped over, still alive. Tereus stabbed him twice more in the chest, killing him instantly.

Realizing what was happening, the second guard took out his sword and pointed it toward the king. He was trembling—more out of confusion than fear.

"Oh, you foolish, stupid man," Tereus shook his head. "You cannot even decide what to do. For that alone, I must kill you."

As Tereus made his move, Procne, Itys, Philomela, and Zafira stood together off to the side. The girl's hands were already free, clutching each other tightly. They watched the scene in shock.

Why is Tereus killing off his own guards?

CHAPTER 27: BEASTS AND MONSTERS

When the guard saw Tereus approaching with his colleague's bloody sword raised, Zafira knew he had to fight or die.

So, fight he did.

Tereus attacked, and the soldier easily defended every one of his blows. It wasn't a very elaborate fight, especially since the perplexed soldier seemed unsure how much strength he should use in a battle with his puny boss. It was straight out of a rehearsal for a Shakespearean play.

They went on for less than a minute when Tereus finally said, "Well done, man. You have passed the trial."

With that, the soldier stopped fighting, sighed, and relaxed his defense.

And in that very second, Tereus—with wild lunacy in his eyes—ran his sword straight into the guard's stomach. The man clutched at the sword impaling him, coughed, and slumped off.

Tereus tittered while using the fallen soldier's tunic to wipe the blood off the blade. He then whipped around to see the group huddled together in a far corner.

"Ah, yes, there you are," he said and cocked his head to the right. "I see you somehow managed to release yourselves." Tereus shrugged. "Certainly, I do not know how, but that is not important. For you see, I would have released you as I said I would. Yet, you must be thinking in those empty little heads of yours: why? Am I correct?"

No one answered. Zafira was still seething and almost trembling in her fury, while Philomela and Procne were visibly tense and on guard.

Tereus jokingly tip-toed toward them in exaggeration and continued his crazy, maniacal speech. "You see, I wanted you to be free to try and fight your way out of what is to come. For me, I will savor seeing you two fight to survive. So, yes, I released you, but that does not mean I will *free* you. NEVER!"

Tereus laughed and went on. "You see, you will both die here, today, in front of my eyes! Further, I could not risk the reflex of my foolish soldiers, who might have fought to protect or save two stupid girls such as yourselves, even if it meant going against my orders. No, the display that is to come is to have no disruption and no other spectators. Only I!"

Zafira's heart thumped in her ears as she feared what he was talking about.

"Ah, perhaps I should have killed you, Philomela, when I had the chance," Tereus said. He sashayed around them, gesturing with the sword while he spoke. "And now that you have become so deformed and disgusting, I realize I should have ended you. The time, however, has now finally come to complete what I started weeks ago." He stopped and glared at Philomela. Then smiled eerily and continued talking and pacing.

"I suspected that you had sent that message to your sister. Certainly, I knew she would search for you — predictable as my dear wife is. So, I moved you to that cave. I assumed either you would starve to death or she would find you. Both possibilities were acceptable to me. Although, you do surprise me slightly, Procne. How you managed to reach your sister was quite unexpected."

The girls stayed huddled, shocked and terrified.

"May I be honest?" Tereus added with a liquidy laugh. He inched closer. "I did hope you would save her so that this very scene would come true! I have envisioned this for several weeks — ever since I made the decision to do away with both of you. Procne, you had become too unbearable with all your weeping and sadness. I knew I had to kill you." He scoffed at Procne and turned back to Philomela.

"Indeed, you as well, Philomela. You see, both of you have served your purpose. I have had my fill of you both and have already obtained the favor I need with the King of Athens. Oh, and he will believe me, without a doubt, when I tell him the story of how you, Procne, slipped off the cliffs one rainy evening. And you, Philomela, slipped when trying to save her. Oh, what a terrible, tragic accident!"

His laugh intensified. He was deliriously insane, and Zafira knew they had to do something. She knew she was there to save them.

"Oh yes, it will be perfect! Truly, the King of Athens would not doubt me. Not I, the king who is father to his own progeny. No, no. For you see, his grandson is here with me, and here he shall stay, which will secure my kingdom's safety, protection, and alliance for years to come."

Itys buried his head deeper into his mother's side as if on cue. He seemed terrified to even look at his own father.

"Now, Itys…stop behaving this way. Come to me! Did

you not enjoy watching your papa defeat those men? A young prince needs to learn how to fight and how to kill. Now, come to me at once, boy! I will not repeat my command!" Tereus giggled again like a lunatic. "You see, my prince, you will want to stay by my side during the performance."

Procne erupted. "He will never come to you again! NEVER!" She shielded Itys behind her and spat at Tereus. The saliva landed in front of him.

Tereus chuckled again and cleared his phlegmy throat, staring at the spit. "That is fine. Let us see if you want him to stay next to you in the next few minutes."

"What? What is it? You...you wretch, you vile creature, you! What will happen?" Procne yelled.

The answer came straight away. But not from Tereus. Instead, a rumbling was heard outside the room. All heads whipped toward the door as something came stomping inside, crouching to make it past the tall entryway.

The girls shrieked.

When the creature stood up to its full height, it was over nine feet tall. Its body had the mass and bulk of a rhinoceros if a rhino could stand upright. But it wasn't gray. It was black—a dark charcoal color.

Its body was furry, with long straggly hair that was clumpy and muddy. The hair stopped at its chin, leaving a bare face and scalp, which was worse. If it had been completely hairy, at least it would have covered the disgusting, red, bumpy, wrinkly face that resembled some of the ugliest hairless animals in the world. Its mouth was also black—a toothless cavern—and, finally, its eyes were reddish yellow. As soon as the creature stood up, it let out a massive roar.

All three girls and Itys screamed again. Tereus just

giggled his crazy laugh.

"Ha! Now you have met my large friend," Tereus said, still snickering. "Certainly, you did not think I would try to kill you myself? Why, I would lose all the value and enjoyment of a spectator. No, my dears, my creature soldier here will take care of the work while I sit back and watch!"

"We've got to get out of here!" Zafira screamed.

Procne scooped up Itys, and they all made for the small doorway in the back—the only unblocked escape.

CHAPTER 28: FIGHT AND FLIGHT

The beast was right on their heels. It reached out to grab Zafira, but she jerked to the side and avoided getting caught.

Procne found an amphora vase nearby and threw it over her shoulder, back toward the creature. It punched it into pieces with its left hand.

Tereus was making disgusting 'mmmm' sounds like he was savoring a delicious meal. He settled onto his throne to watch the massacre.

The girls made it into the storeroom, but it was a dead end.

"Quick, retreat before we are trapped," Procne cried out.

It was already too late. The monster filled up the entire doorway behind them. It let out a horrible bellow and a snort.

"Start throwing stuff at it!" Zafira yelled. She grabbed a nearby terracotta jug. Procne and Philomela did the same, and within seconds they were attacking the beast with every type of vase, bowl, pitcher, and vessel they could find and heave.

Of course, this did nothing to the monster. But somehow, while dodging non-stop flying objects, it moved backward—just a little. And kept moving back. Plus, like many enormous animals, it was big but slow.

So, as soon as the doorway was clear enough, Zafira and Procne—with Itys on her back—nimbly rushed out and back into the center of the giant room. Philomela, the last to try to squeeze past, wasn't as lucky. The beast grabbed her with both arms and threw her across the room.

"Philomela!" Procne screamed. They all ran toward her.

Philomela was shaken but not hurt, which was a miracle considering how frail she was.

Zafira knew her invisibility was their only hope. The beast was coming fast. "Try to keep it distracted," she panted to the girls beside her. "I'll get Tereus!"

Zafira ran over to the tiny king and did the first thing that came to mind. She started pulling and yanking at his clothes. Tereus seemed shocked and surprised, wondering what was happening. He swatted at the air.

Zafira got more aggressive. She had obviously never pushed, slapped, or hit a grown man—or anyone for that matter—before. But as soon as she thought about all the pain and damage this loser had done to those two innocent girls, the rage she had been stifling before finally boiled over.

She had turned into a superhero once or twice previously in her dreams. But this time, she was still Zafira, just letting loose some of the most forceful, heavy hits and punches that had probably ever come out of a ten-year-old.

Tereus was beyond agitated and nervous. He was actually getting hurt. He tried punching, slapping, and flailing at the air around him. But without a sword and without tricks, he was powerless and weak.

"I do not know what you are or who sent you," Tereus

yelled. "But you cannot harm me!"

Meanwhile, the princesses were trying to bob and weave around the monster. Procne had tucked Itys safely away in a corner. They were both using all their strength to fight. But they knew they were no match for the beast. It was way too big and way too strong.

"What can we do?" Procne yelled to her sister. "We will be killed by this beast!"

Philomela noticed a nearby oil lamp. She crouched down in time to avoid the creature's swipe and rolled over to grab it. She flung it right into the monster's eyes. It shrieked at the searing pain from the burning oil.

Procne then saw her own chance and lunged for another lamp. She used hers to light the monster's leg hair on fire. The creature instantly patted it out while still groaning. But that was all it took for the girls to see what they needed to do to beat it.

"Fire!" Procne yelled. "Burn it up!!"

Together, they ignited different parts of the monster. They kept at it—one right after the other. While the beast was busy putting out one, another part of its hairy body would already be burning.

Soon—and with the help of a huge draft running through the big room—the monster was flailing about, completely engulfed in flames.

Tereus, who had been so distracted by his invisible attack, looked shocked at what had happened to his creature. The monster had already crumbled to the ground. It was an immobile mound that continued to burn.

When Tereus spotted the two sisters huddled in a corner, cradling Itys between them, he let out a roar and lunged toward them. With Itys in Procne's arms, the girls jumped up, screaming, and ran away. Zafira raced from behind—punching, pulling, and tripping up Tereus.

The wild chase spilled out from the enormous central room, through its porched entrance, and across a nearby courtyard. There were stunned guards and soldiers all around, but no one moved to stop them. It was like they knew this scene had to play out without anyone interrupting.

The group sprinted through several corridors, around curvy columns, and finally out into an enormous outdoor square. Zafira's assaults were doing nothing to slow Tereus down. If anything, they aggravated and infuriated him into going faster. He was gaining on the sisters.

The square had a colonnade and a large set of steps that went up to the walkway on the fortified wall surrounding the entire palace. The girls went straight for the stairs.

Procne slipped but stayed upright, and Itys was locked in her firm, protective embrace. Philomela strayed a little behind. It was like she wanted to be the first one Tereus would attack.

They raced up the steps, two at a time.

Where are they going?

"Girls!" Zafira hollered. "Why don't we all attack him together?" They didn't seem to hear her.

The girls kept pushing upward. Philomela and Procne were so focused on their escape—so consumed by going on and going up—they almost looked like they were floating in their retreat.

Tereus was also picking up speed, but Zafira was slowing down. She couldn't keep up!

"Philomela! Procne!! Wait! I can't reach you...I can't help you! Where are you going?" Zafira's lungs burned, and sweat blinded her. She wanted to stick together but couldn't shake the feeling that the girls had another plan—just the two of them and Itys.

Zafira couldn't go faster. It was like she was wearing a backpack with a bowling ball in it. She was moving, but barely.

The girls had already made it up to the top of the wall and were now running along it. The palace was below them on their right, and the sea sprawled out on their left. Tereus was still in pursuit. Zafira, though, had to stop when she got to the top. She was panting and wheezing.

But the girls dashed on ahead. They were racing right on the edge of the wall, high up over the cliffs below. Zafira shuddered. It was too dangerous. She'd have to stop them soon.

That was when everything happened—in a flash and in slow motion simultaneously. Zafira could only stand by and watch.

First, Tereus accelerated even more, reached Philomela, and grabbed her loose, shapeless dress. Without stopping or breaking stride, Philomela ripped it off her and left it behind in Tereus's fist. She was now running bare-chested with a light beige slip covering her lower half. Tereus threw the dress to the left, and Zafira saw it float down into the crashing waves below.

Philomela caught up to Procne again, but Tereus was right behind them. Up ahead, the wall veered to the right to enclose the western side of the palace. But the girls didn't turn right. They didn't follow the wall.

Instead, they gazed at each other lovingly, Procne grabbed Philomela's hand while still holding onto Itys, and they all turned to the left. They sped up and floated right off the side of the wall—high up and over the sea.

Tereus didn't stop running or chasing them either. In fact, he was so consumed by the chase that the creep didn't even realize he had also run out of space. The idiot king had launched himself out over the edge as well.

"Girls?!" Zafira shrieked. "Wait! No!" Zafira finally reached the point where all four had run off the wall. But in the very second, when she expected to see them falling down, plunging to their death, the most unusual thing happened.

All four were instantly transformed into birds.

Procne and Itys, still hugging, turned into nightingales while Philomela evaporated into a swallow. As soon as all three were together, they quickly flew away.

Tereus was also transformed into a bird, but a small, ugly one. He couldn't chase them anymore since they could fly much faster. So, he glided and slowly drifted away.

Zafira stared out into the distance in disbelief, unable to understand what had just happened and where the girls had gone.

"Philomela!! Procne!!" She yelled out into the vast blue ahead of her. Of course, there was no reply. Zafira fell to her knees, sobbing.

Behind her, she heard several guards call out, "Halt! You there! Do not move!"

She spun around. At least six guards were coming right toward her. They could see her now!

Well, I guess it would be a...a...a near-death...near-death...death?! But how? Maybe now...

But Zafira's head was too light, and darkness swooped in from every side. She was falling into a dark hole. The last things she saw before passing out were those three birds flying off into the horizon.

CHAPTER 29: REUNITED AND UNITED

Zafira's eyes fluttered open. She jerked up and looked around.

She wasn't in bed.

I'm still in the dream! But where am I?

The wall was gone. The sea was gone. Zafira was outside somewhere, but she was no longer on the fortified palace wall. She was sitting on a dirt path. Behind her, a temple was being reconstructed—a temple with three distinctive doors.

The temple on the Acropolis!

She recognized it right away. They must have already started rebuilding it, which meant she was back in Athens. And now she knew it was Mycenaean Athens! She stood up, wiping the dust and sand off.

Her mind flashed back to the girls running off the wall and turning into birds.

Why did they do that? And now what? Why am I back here?

Her mind was a blur as she trudged down the same path she and Philomela had run down after the earthquake only a few days ago. Well, it had been days for *her* but years for everyone else.

She decided to head toward the palace. But as she got closer to the entrance, she came across King Pandion coming up from the Snake Gate.

The king had three soldiers surrounding him. He seemed much older and more tired than she had seen him before. He plodded along, hunched over. His face was sunken and sullen.

Zafira froze. She realized she might not be invisible anymore since the guards in the other palace were able to see her. Thankfully though, they walked right passed her—oblivious.

As they passed, she overheard the king ask one of the men, "I do not understand. How can this be true? How could they have become *birds*?"

"It is true, my king. Many of Tereus's..."

"DO NOT EVER SPEAK THAT NAME TO ME!!" The king roared, and the soldier cowered.

"Please, forgive me, sir," the soldier bowed and slowly continued. "Many of...erm...*his* soldiers and guards were on the wall when the event happened. They bore witness. They saw that the young queen and the prince became nightingales, and the princess became a swallow...erm...as for him...he became a small, slow, and quite foul hoopoe."

"It is too much! Is it true that he had kept my youngest daughter a prisoner, had treated my oldest so terribly, and, in the end, he wanted to kill them all?" His voice was heavy with agony. "Oh, wretched me! How could I let this happen? Why did I not protect them?"

The king tried to swallow his sobs. Zafira sympathized with the man's pain and anguish. Right now, he was a grieving father more than a king.

The soldier fidgeted in discomfort and was unable to tactfully respond. "It is true, my king. The messenger guards who arrived this morning left his kingdom by ship as soon as possible to quickly bring this to your attention. Many guards and other servants shared the information they all individually knew or observed in the weeks before the event. Then, when two soldiers' bodies were discovered murdered by Ter—by him, there was no loyalty left. They swiftly informed the messengers, who are here now. The soldiers, guards, and servants are all unified in their grief and guilt for having chosen cowardly obedience over justice and protection for your beautiful daughters. For that, we are all so deeply sorry."

The king was beyond distraught. "Yet, what of that strange, young girl they say appeared on the wall during the event?"

"It was very unusual, indeed. She emerged from the air and disappeared just as quickly. No one knows who she was or where she went. Many guards think she may have been acting on behalf of the gods. In fact, most witnesses agree that what happened to Procne, Philomela, and Itys can only have been performed by the gods."

"The gods?" The king gaped at the soldier like he was insane. "But why? Why must they take my two girls, and my grandson, away from me? They just flew away!!" The king seemed like he couldn't—and maybe didn't—want to hold it in anymore. He dismissed the soldiers with a hasty wave and stumbled back to his palace alone. He wept with every step.

They were really gone.

And I didn't save them after all!

Zafira's sadness engulfed her. This was going to be one of the worst dreams ever. It was becoming a nightmare, and she *never* planned those.

King Pandion faded further into the distance. She felt for him and wished there was a way to help. But deep inside, she knew her time in ancient Greece had come to an end. It was time to wake up.

As she staggered through the main gate, she turned back one last time to look at the Mycenaean Acropolis, which she would never forget. It would forever hold a piece of Zafira's own history, and she couldn't wait to tell Yaya everything.

She walked through the outskirts, chanting to wake herself up, but the dream continued. Just as she was starting to wonder why, she saw several little birds zipping out of the trees to her left.

In seconds, she was surrounded by four birds. They chirped, swooped, and flittered all around her.

Zafira knew right away that they were, of course, two nightingales, a beautiful swallow, and a bird with a unique light blue patch on top of its head.

"Philomela, Procne, Itys, and Mr. Bird? Is it really you?" Her voice cracked.

The chirps were incessant, and Zafira knew she was right.

"Oh, thank god! You came to see me? I was so sad! What happened? Are you alright?" Zafira didn't know what kind of reply to expect now that they were birds.

But, to her surprise, one of the nightingales did talk. Zafira figured it had to be Procne. She sang her answer in a beautiful birdsong:

> "Zafira dear, do not worry,
> We are free, full of flurry.
> You have helped in every way,
> Given us peace and our allay."

"Oh, that's so pretty. Is it really you, Procne?" Zafira asked, and Procne chirped back.

"It's so great to see you and...um...sort of talk to you again!" Zafira's smile broadened, peeling away her worry and sadness with it.

The nightingale continued:

"Yes, it is I, and Philomela, too,
We needed to see, and warmly thank you.
We feared you were sad, with worry, and upset,
So, we flew to you to certainly offset.
Any thoughts or doubts that you were to blame,
You are who saved us, who helped, we proclaim."

"Thank me? But you aren't *girls* anymore. You can't go back home and be with your family. You're birds, which is nice and beautiful and everything, but I didn't help you if you couldn't stay the same."

Procne was quick to respond:

"Yes, you did, of this never feel doubt,
We are so happy, love flying about.
Alas, it is true; we will miss our family,
Yet, we will not miss life's other reality."

"Well, yeah, I guess, in a way, that's true. You don't have any rules that you have to follow. And I bet it must be fun to fly around and go wherever you want. So, maybe you guys are freer as birds than girls or princesses." Zafira smiled.

She suddenly remembered Tereus. "You don't happen

to see a small, kind of ugly bird following you around, do you?"

The birds all chirped and tweeted jovially before Procne replied:

> "No, he is gone, with others of his kind,
> We fly together, have nothing to mind.
> From up high and low,
> We see lands close and distant.
> We could never have dreamt,
> Of this lovely existence."

"Well, then...I guess that's really great, Procne. Wait, can Philomela talk and sing too?" Zafira gazed hopefully toward the swallow.

I miss her voice!

> "No, my dear, I am sorry to say, she cannot,
> Not in song, as I do, but for this, fear is naught.
> For she chirps and sings in her own lovely way,
> Happier now than, indeed, ever before today."

With that, the swallow fluttered around Zafira, landed on her shoulder, and chirped happily. Her carefree joy was contagious.

"Wow! Well, I guess it's all okay." Zafira replied, still getting used to the idea. "I'm so relieved that you're all so happy and safe and...together! And is Itys alright too? He doesn't miss being a little boy?"

> "Itys is happy and adapted to his wing,
> Yet he is still a rambunctious fledgling.
> I find him in mud puddles, feathers a mess,

But I am so happy; he is so very careless."

Itys tweeted and darted all around Zafira.
Well, he did want to fly. So, there he goes! Zafira chuckled at his silly style.

"And what about Mr. Bird?" Zafira nodded at her first feathered friend.

"Mr. Bird took the god's instruction,
To guide you straight to Philo's abduction.
As birds, you should know, we actually hear,
Messages from a land not quite near here.
And one more thing, between you and me,
Mr. Bird is not male, for, indeed, she's a she."

"Oh, sorry, Mr....I mean, Ms. Bird! I didn't know!" Zafira giggled. "But wait...you said she got a message from the gods? Which gods? Was it Athena? Was she helping all along? Was that who also sent the falcon and helped in those other ways? And was Zeus really out to get us? Did he help Tereus and send all those creatures? But what about at the end..." Zafira's mind was racing.

The birds were chirping while Zafira went on. "And the prophecy? Was it all part of some plan? Was it—" But Zafira was interrupted by Procne, who had landed on her shoulder and was cooing in her ear. It tickled, and Zafira laughed.

Guess I'll have to wonder. And really, who cares anymore. Zafira smiled and nuzzled Procne, ready to wake up. *It's all over!*

"I guess it's time to say bye," Zafira said gloomily.
Procne's coos turned to the song:

"Do not be sad, our dearest friend,

We love you and will always blend,
Into your life, even when unseen,
Maybe in real life, or just a dream."

Zafira gasped. She had never told them. Did they already know? Did it matter?

"Thank you, Procne. I'll always remember you, too—all of you. And I'll miss you...A LOT!"

"We, too, are so happy, and so we bid,
Farewell, good luck, and happiness amid,
A life full of love and so much success,
And only good things, to you, we all bless!"

Then, the nightingale chirped a lovely birdsong while nestling against Zafira's cheek and neck. Next, Philomela flew down and nuzzled her as well. She sang with her own chirps and tweets, tickling and trilling Zafira's ears.

"Oh, Philomela, I'm going to miss you. We've been through a lot! And you don't know this, but thank you for teaching me so much." Zafira shuddered. "And goodbye, Ms. Bird."

One by one, the birds took turns on Zafira's shoulder. They all caressed and cuddled her. Zafira kissed and patted each bird in turn. In the end, Philomela rested once more on Zafira's shoulder, and Zafira gave her one last long kiss on top of her tiny, furry head.

Then—poof. Darkness swooped all around her again, and that was that. Her dream was finally over.

CHAPTER 30: MYTHS AND LEGENDS

Zafira woke up with a start. Her pillow was soaked.

Gross! I must have been sweating up a storm!

She got up and went to open her shades. It was still light out.

What time is it?

Zafira quickly changed into jeans and a T-shirt and ran downstairs. Yaya was reading at the kitchen table with a bowl of half-eaten fruit salad in front of her.

"Oh, Zaffy! You're up. How do you feel?"

Zafira rushed up to her grandma and gave her a tight hug.

"Whoa. That's great, *gliki mou*, but what's up?"

Zafira grabbed Yaya's fork and stabbed at a sliced-up strawberry.

"Yaya, I'm feeling great!" she exclaimed with a huge smirk. "And I have the *best* dream to tell you about!"

***

After Zafira had finished her story, Yaya's expression was full of shock...and a little pride.

"Well, Zaffy, I must admit, that is some dream. But there is no way you could have known all that stuff, even with everything I told you before your nap. I definitely didn't go into that much detail, and I surely never mentioned Philomela and Procne."

Yaya looked really skeptical. "Hold on a sec, sweetie." She got up and went into Stelios's study. Zafira trailed from behind.

It took Yaya a few minutes to search her son's bookshelf, but she eventually found a book and carried it to his sturdy oak desk. The two sat side-by-side while Yaya flipped through the pages.

She came across a list. "Here's a list of some of the legendary rulers of Athens. See, King Pandion was one of many Athenian rulers who was said to have even descended from the mythological gods. But this book says we can't be sure of when they ruled. Maybe it was way before the Mycenaeans or maybe even around that time."

Yaya scratched her head, her expression full of suspicion. "Before King Pandion, there was King Erichthonios who was believed to have been the son of Hephaistos and Athena via Gaia...but, it's just like what you said, Zaffy. How is this possible? Have you been listening to your dad prepare his lectures or something?"

Zafira shrugged. "I mean, maybe? I guess we'll have to ask Dad later. But wait, Yaya, this keeps talking about legends and myths. What's the difference?"

"Great question, Zafira. Well, in the simplest sense, legends are usually oral stories passed on from generation to generation. They contain lots of important messages and lessons from that culture. Also, legends are supposed to hold some elements of truth. But, as you know from when you played the telephone game when you were younger, the longer a story is passed on from person to person, the 'truth' gets mixed up along the way. Basically, legends are supposed to have some truth somewhere in them, but they usually can't be verified or proven."

Zafira nodded slowly, and Yaya went on. "Myths, on the other hand, are traditional stories about a culture's origins. So, for the ancient Greeks, they included the gods, for example, Zeus and Athena, and stories of where they came from, like Gaia, which means 'earth,' and Uranos, which means 'sky.' So, you see, the myths talk about how the ancient Greeks were born from the earth and the sky."

Suddenly, Yaya gasped and pointed to another page in the book. "Look, Zaffy. Procne and Philomela!" Her grandma scanned the text.

"Oh, but this is a bit shocking, sweetie."

"Why?" Zafira asked. She obviously couldn't read as fast as her grandma.

"Well, it does have a nice ending, but just promise you won't tell your parents what I'm about to tell you, okay?" Zafira nodded enthusiastically and urged her grandma to go on.

"So, according to this, there have been different stories and interpretations about the princesses, but one of the most famous came from a Roman poet named Ovid, who lived around a thousand five hundred years *after* the Mycenaeans."

Yaya recounted a story that almost mirrored Zafira's dream, including Procne, Tereus, Itys, Philomela's journey up to Thrace, Tereus cutting out Philomela's tongue and keeping her prisoner, and, finally, ending in Philomela's woven message to Procne.

"My goodness, Zaffy, it's all like what you dreamt! Except when Procne got the message that Philomela was alive, she snuck out of the castle by dressing up in disguise during a seasonal festival, and she found and saved her sister from the castle, not a cave. But honey, that's where the similarities end because then..." Yaya cleared her throat. "Well, the legend really takes a gross turn."

"What? What happened, Yaya?"

"So, remember now, Zaffy, this is all legend, and sometimes these stories can get a bit...erm...gruesome. Anyway, apparently, Procne was so mad at Tereus that she wanted to get her revenge on him. The first person she saw was her little son, who looked so much like Tereus. And so, in a moment of absolute rage, Procne killed Itys and then...umm...cooked the baby—boiled him and served him to Tereus for dinner. Horrible, right?"

Zafira gasped. "But that's not what happened in my dream!"

"I know, but then this part was: when Tereus found out what he had eaten, he got so mad that he chased both sisters out of the house, and I guess he chased them both off a cliff. And he fell, too. Except they didn't fall; they all transformed into birds. Philomela turned into a swallow, Tereus into a small, not really pretty bird called a hoopoe, and Procne into a nightingale...you know, the bird that sings? And they say she would sing her sad story night after night."

"The birds!" Zafira gasped. "It's true, even in the legend! Except for that horrible part with Procne. She'd never do that!"

"Well, after that, they say the king was so sad that he died of grief. His son, the girls' brother Erectheos, became the next King of Athens. And on it goes. But the girls *did* turn into beautiful birds. Wow!" Yaya exhaled, shaking her head slowly in apparent disbelief.

"Yaya, don't you see? The girls became famous in Athenian history. But with lots of wrong parts! I don't want people to remember Procne this way. She would have never done something so horrible. And the way it was being remembered almost made it so that the prophecy had been right."

"Zaffy, you're talking like this all happened. Sweetie, remember, it was all a dream."

"But it was so real...too real. And you can't believe how I knew some of this stuff, so maybe—"

"Maybe nothing, *koukla mou.*" Yaya shut the book and stood up, taking Zafira's hand to lead her out of the study.

"Listen, darling, you've had quite a night and quite a day. I love how creative and imaginative your dreams are becoming, and I'm thrilled you can plan these amazing adventures, but they aren't real, hon."

"But, Yaya, how could my brain come up with all those details and all that stuff that actually happened? And how could I *feel* all the pain and stuff?"

"Well, honey, our subconscious is powerful and mysterious." Yaya chuckled and ruffled Zafira's hair. "Now, come on, Zaffy... Let's get that journal of yours. You can write it all up while I fix some dinner for us to eat with your parents tonight. Then we'll ask your dad what he makes of it, okay?"

***

Part of the mystery was solved over dinner that night when Stelios explained that he had been preparing a lecture on Roman interpretations of earlier Greek legends. But how Zafira had overheard or absorbed all the information she knew was ultimately a puzzle.

The strangest part was that Stelios had never told Zafira about Philomela and Procne. But somehow, she knew!

While helping her grandma with the dishes later that evening, Zafira's mind was still racing.

"Maybe I've got, like, psychic powers...but only in my dreams," she said excitedly. "But instead of seeing the future, I can see the past. But, like, *really* see it, and live it, and know it!"

Yaya chuckled. "Okay there, Nostradamus."

"Who's that?"

"A guy from the past who was famous for being able to tell the future."

Zafira frowned. "But, Yaya, I still don't know why I would dream a dream like this?"

"Well, sweetie, even though we don't know *how* you dreamt this, I think I know *why*. See, besides needing all that excitement and adventure, I think you've come to learn a lesson that has been very important in my life and actually one of the reasons I became an art historian."

"What's that, Yaya?" Zafira asked and put the last glass in the dishwasher.

Yaya wiped her hands on a towel and turned to Zafira.

"That it's really worthwhile to look back to past cultures to learn, not only what they thought was beautiful and artistic, but also to see how they lived, what they valued, and what they loved."

Zafira smiled and nodded slowly. Yaya added, "You know, the past can teach us a lot about ourselves now, in the present. I mean, didn't you learn a lot in your dream, Zaffy?"

Zafira cocked her head. "I guess, yeah...I did!" She giggled. "Like, how far I'd go to help a friend."

Yaya smiled and beamed. "And you know, honey, all your dreams come from right here," she tapped Zafira on the side of the head. "And, you know what we call this part of your head, right *koukla mou?*"

Zafira's eyes bulged out. "My temple!" She gasped.

Yaya chuckled sweetly. "That's right...that's your temple, my love."

"My own temple! Like Athena's temple?" Zafira scrunched her face, and they both laughed.

"Kind of. And you've got two of them; one on the left and one on the right. Your own magical temples that will keep you dreaming beautifully and dreaming big! Promise me, you won't ever stop planning those dream adventures, right Zaffy?"

"Of course not, Yaya!" Zafira turned and took her dream journal off of the counter. Then, with a sly smile, Zafira added, "Like, what was that thing you told me about once...about that Runny-sauce time..."

Yaya laughed. "The Renaissance? Oh, Zaffy, let's get you upstairs and ready for bed!"

The End

AUTHOR'S NOTE

This is a work of fiction. That's true, but many of the names, characters, places, events, locales, and incidents are *not* just the product of my imagination and are *not* used only in a fictitious manner. And any resemblance to actual persons, living or dead, or actual events was *not* purely coincidental.

In fact, months of research went into providing as many historical, art historical, and mythological details as possible. Of course, when dealing with a time period that is so far in the past—and during which not much was kept as a written record—well, creative liberty was obviously used to help connect some dots and to help elaborate my fictional tale. Still, I aimed to write a *fantasy* book that would bring *real* art historical facts and information to young readers, and I hope I succeeded. But Zafira's part in this story only scratches the (colorful) surface of ancient Greek art.

So, reader (young or not-so-young), I encourage you to discover more by looking up (among other related topics): the art and culture of the Mycenaeans, the Bronze Age, the early age of Greece (its architecture, sculpture, vases, and other artifacts), ancient Athens, Greek gods and heroes, Homer, The Trojan War, and (of course) the myth of Philomela and Procne.

There's a lot more to learn, and that's what makes art history so fascinating. It's what art and architecture can tell us about the people, places, things, culture, religion, beliefs, lifestyles, landscapes, food, work, education, entertainment, and so many other aspects of a society that existed centuries before us. But, from there, nothing stops us from letting our imaginations (and maybe even our dreams) take over.

ACKNOWLEDGMENTS

I am so grateful to all the wonderful, supportive, and loving people in my life who encourage me in unique ways every day. I am truly a better person because of each of you.

Thanks go, first and foremost, to my parents, Therese and Nicolas, for being my eternal fans and for always believing in me. Also, thank you to Phil, Val, Niko, Theo, and Ana for your caring love and support and for inspiring me to return to story-telling. Thanks to Evelyn for always providing great suggestions, advice, and comfort. And many additional thanks to all the other amazing people who, through it all, helped fuel my creative fire, including Andrea, Rosi, Ezio, my own Yaya, Ketty, Vicky, Beth, Daniela, Natalie, Naomi, Emily, and Roisin. There truly aren't enough words to express all of my gratitude. Finally, a special thanks to my mom for her beautiful cover art and to Giuseppe for his eleventh-hour help with the cover.

ABOUT THE AUTHOR

Eugenie Makrogiannis was born in Montreal, Canada, moved to Greece as a young child, but grew up in San Diego, California—her true hometown. She has also lived in Seattle, San Francisco, and Los Angeles but currently resides near Lake Como in Northern Italy.

She studied journalism at the University of Washington and art history at UC Davis. She now teaches English as a Foreign Language in Italy. She is a proud aunt to three amazing kids and loves traveling, reading, watching addictive TV shows, swimming in the Aegean Sea, and exploring new places. *Zafira and the Birds* is her first novel, but she hopes Zafira will have many more dream adventures in the future.